Wrong Side of the River

They destroyed Connery's livelihood when they wrecked his riverboat. Not only that, they killed one of his crewmen at the same time. Connery knew enough about the river that you didn't let such things pass without trying to square them. But he had more enemies than he figured, and they hit him with a whole bunch of dirty tricks.

Which was their mistake. Connery knew plenty of tricks of his own. He oiled his guns, flexed his fists, and the bodies stretched from Laredo clear down to the Hermoso valley before he was through. Connery sure was a tough hombre!

Wrong Side of the River

TYLER HATCH

A Black Horse Western

ROBERT HALE · LONDON

© Tyler Hatch 2004
First published in Great Britain 2004

ISBN 0 7090 7590 1

Robert Hale Limited
Clerkenwell House
Clerkenwell Green
London EC1R 0HT

Typeset by
Derek Doyle & Associates, Liverpool.
Printed and bound in Great Britain by
Antony Rowe Limited, Wiltshire

CHAPTER 1

SHOESTRING OUTFIT

It was this way: there had been wild weather further up-river and the Pecos poured thousands of gallons of extra muddy water and as many thousands of tons of silt into the Rio Grande. Lake Amistad had filled to capacity and beyond and the overflow went down-stream, causing strong, fast currents and a build up of sand bars way down near Laredo.

It was one of these muscular currents that grabbed the modified keelboat *Rio Belle* just north of Laredo and pushed it relentlessly towards the American side of the river. Sail power was useless against such force.

The Negro, Ruben, and the kid deckhand, Ace, were in the bows, swinging the lead lines constantly.

'Mark twain!' roared Ruben's deep African voice.

'About the same – little more!' piped Ace, not yet

out of his teens and sure to be a runaway from somewhere. But a good worker.

McAllen was standing by the single mast, ready to move on the order of Captain Clay Connery who was fighting the kicking and jumping of the heavy tiller alone in the stern. Above Mac the square sail flapped and cracked, spilling some of the wind.

'Lower sail, Mac!' Connery roared, his shirt soaked and showing the cut of his muscles across his chest and in his upper arms. He was bareheaded and spray had plastered his thick black hair in streaks down his wolfish face. 'Slowly. The sail's useless now but the wind'll change any minute.'

'In a pig's eye!' Mac murmured, not loud enough for Connery to hear, but he began to fight the sail down.

Ruben glanced at Connery who nodded and the Negro went to help the struggling McAllen.

The way dropped off the heavy boat and she rocked on the ripple of the first sandbar. Ace screamed there were more ahead, suddenly appearing out of surging, chocolate-coloured waves that lifted the hull. At the same time, he looked back beyond the straining Connery and pointed, face going pale.

'Oh, my God, Skipper! Behind us!'

Connery glanced over his left shoulder and felt his guts knot. There was a huge sternwheel steamboat bearing down on them, bow wave white and high. The whistle clamoured urgently, arrogantly, and the man in the wheelhouse leaned out the window. Even from here Connery could see the contemptuous grin on Keller's square face.

WRONG SIDE OF THE RIVER

'You're workin' the wrong side of the river, Connery, me lad!' the steamer man bellowed, his words just reaching the *Rio Belle* above all the splashing and creaking as the keelboat grounded and rolled violently.

McAllen and Ruben had paused in lowering the sail and the keelboat rocked and canted. Connery didn't bother answering Keller, but he kept an eye on the giant *Blade* as the man eased his helm and angled in towards the *Belle*.

'Oh, Judas, Skipper! He's – he's gonna ram us!' Ace looked as if he was getting ready to dive over the side but Connery knew the boy couldn't swim very well and would think twice about it. Such a move would be pure desperation on Ace's part . . . then Connery made his own desperate move.

'Up sail!' he bawled. If they had to ground, they might as well do it properly and keep the boat from being carried out of control down-river with planks stove-in. And it would be too shallow for the steamboat to reach them, if that was Keller's plan. . . .

The weathered canvas swung part way round the mast, then suddenly bellied with a crack like a rifleshot as a gust of wind caught it. At the same time, Connery threw all his weight against the long, heavy tiller bar, his feet almost leaving the deck as he grunted with effort, trying to keep the bows towards the bank now. One more gust like that and they would be laid on their beam ends.

The mast shuddered and the rope burned through McAllen's hands but he didn't even take time to curse. He swung his weight on the line in

7

unison with Ruben – they had worked together for months now and could almost read each other's minds in situations like this.

'Make fast!' bellowed Connery, as their efforts hauled the squaresail higher. They looked surprised but instantly obeyed like the good sailors they were.

The keelboat heeled and creaked and Ace grabbed wildly at a flailing line to steady himself, running back to the bow as Connery roared an order. He braced himself and reached for the leadline. He glanced over his shoulder and his eyes widened as he watched the *Blade*, pride of King's fleet of twenty paddle steamers, swing her giant, twenty-five-foot diameter sternwheel towards the *Belle*.

'*No-o-o-o!*' he cried as loud as he could when he saw the huge wheel suddenly thrash the river to foam and floating mud and debris were torn from the bottom by the massive surge, as Keller deliberately powered-up. Black smoke belched from the *Blade*'s tall stacks. He could hear the metallic working of straining bearings and con-rods, the roar of high pressure steam. The boat shuddered with the abrupt effort to change speed, hung-up, poised to leap forward, but that was just what Keller wanted. While it was suspended before the lunge into the current, the bigger boat's wash ripped the river into waves that slapped across the keelboat's deck, tilted her dangerously – forcing the *Rio Belle* across the sand-bars sideways, rocking and scraping and lurching.

She struck with a deep, rending shudder and the mast snapped, trapping McAllen and Ruben in a tangle of rope and canvas. The deck cargo shifted, its

weight snapping the tie-down ropes one by one, cant-
ing the boat dangerously. Ace catapulted violently
from the bows and disappeared beneath the swirling,
raging waters. If he cried out no one heard him.

Connery slammed heavily into stacked bales, his
head striking a bracing plank. Stars exploded and
warm blood washed over his face as he fell, sliding
down the tilted deck, striking the gunwale briefly
before splashing into the churning river.

He sank, surfaced, glimpsed the blades of the
thrashing sternwheel only yards away, and then he
was swamped by grit-laden waves that almost choked
him, the surge painfully wrenching at his limbs. He
submerged again, partly voluntarily, for he knew he
couldn't survive in that maelstrom above. Choking,
he shot to the surface, arms tearing at the air, half-
blinded with silt, gagging and spitting. His half boots
had filled and were dragging him down but he felt
the soggy sandbar beneath him and floundered more
or less upright. Lucky they weren't shipping any
steers, this trip, he thought wildly as he waded around
the wrecked boat. Being in this mess of waters with
panicked cattle was not a situation to contemplate.

He clawed grit out of his eyes, saw the *Blade* heading on up river now, its steam-driven power easily
pushing it against the down-river surge that had
caused the trouble for the *Belle.*

Keller was out on the roof of the Texas deck, above
the crew's accommodation, waving his seaman's cap
and grinning ear-to-ear.

'Sorry – can't stop to help! Urgent cargo! But
you'll be all right – only a few yards to shore!'

He tugged the cord. The whistle shrilled derisively.

'That big Irish bastard! No wonder they call him "Killer" Keller!' yelled McAllen, shaking his fist after the *Blade*. 'Blast you, you son of a bitch!'

Connery, holding to the splintered gunwale that was awash, saw McAllen and Ruben wading towards him, both men bleeding in several places from wounds received in the stranding.

'Blast King, too!' McAllen said venomously.

But Connery knew Richard King, owner of the Texas ranch that was destined to become the largest cattle spread in the whole country, and eventually home of the Santa Gertrudis cattle breed, hadn't ordered them run aground. King was a tough and sometimes ruthless man but, with his new partner, Miflin Kenedy, another ex-riverboat captain like himself, now managing the fleet of twenty steamboats King operated on the Rio, he was concentrating on his ranch. He had allowed Connery to operate his converted keelboat on the Rio, as long as he worked the Mexican side only, carrying the small consignments King felt were too unprofitable for him.

'We're no risk to King,' Connery told McAllen. 'This was Keller's own idea.'

McAllen squinted curiously at Connery. 'What is it between you and Keller? He's the only one of King's captains who goes out of his way to hassle us.'

'Just the miserable kind of son of a bitch he is.'

McAllen wasn't satisfied, but before he could say more, Ruben suddenly asked urgently, 'Where's Ace?' – and they only then realized the youth wasn't with them.

10

They quickly made their way towards the bows, the boat lying over on the port beam now. Water slopped into their faces, washed about their waists, making progress difficult. There was no sign of the boy. Connery submerged, hoping against hope that maybe Ace had floundered ashore to safety . . . Ruben dived away to the left . . . McAllen, face awash in the river, groped blindly. Minutes ticked by. No one could survive underwater that long, Connery knew.

'Cap'n!'

Connery snapped his head around at the deep-throated call by Ruben. He slowly released the breath and staggered to his feet, clawing at his eyes.

He held a small limp body, the flesh wet and white, arms and head dangling loosely, the lank sandy hair that had annoyed the hell out of Connery for the last couple of weeks plastered over the gaunt face, masked now with blood. Ace's mouth was full of silt, his nostrils clogged with it.

They got him to shore – there were no spectators, no one to help, as this part of the river was uninhabited and Laredo lay a couple of miles away. Connery knew a little first aid from the War and laid the lad head down over a log, placed his hands on his lower ribs and worked forwards and backwards, alternately applying pressure on the forward stroke, easing up on the backward. Water ran out of the boy's mouth and sucking air made grunting, wheezing noises, but they were not the sounds of returning life.

Ace had drowned. And even if the water hadn't done for him, likely the deep wound on his head would have.

'Kid didn't stand a chance,' allowed McAllen, grimly.

Connery lifted the dead youth into his arms and looked at Ruben. 'You stay and keep an eye on things, Rube – not that there's much you can do.'

'I can stop some of them baulks of timber floatin' away, Skipper.'

'Don't go getting yourself crushed by 'em,' warned Connery. 'Keep any looters away as best you can. Mac, let's start for Laredo.'

McAllen didn't move. He was a medium-built man with a long face and a square, jutting jaw. His big scarred fists curled down at his sides.

'Our guns are still in the deckhouse – I can get 'em. They'll dry out by the time we get to town.'

'Leave 'em. Rube can get 'em if he needs 'em.'

McAllen was shocked. 'You're gonna go after Keller, for Chris'sakes!'

'He's headed up-river, Mac. He'll go all the way to Del Rio, likely. We'll catch up with him – he's got to come back down some time.'

Mac's lips curled. 'Meanwhile – what?'

'Meanwhile, we get Ace to town and see about a decent burial for him. Then we make arrangements to salvage what freight we can. Customers in Brownsville and Matamoros will be waiting.'

Rube and McAllen both knew that Connery was a man of his word, always saw any undertaking through to the end, no matter what. Even though the river freight company was a shoestring operation, they had a good reputation because of Connery's ethics.

'How we gonna do that?' McAllen wanted to know.

'Gonna be tight, but guess we'll have to hire wagons, drive 'em overland – unless we can save the boat.'

McAllen and Ruben both turned and looked at the splintered wreck of the *Rio Belle*.

McAllen, with his usual pessimism, stared levelly at Connery. 'What boat?' he asked grimly.

CHAPTER 2

THE RIO BELLE

Carrying the dead boy, but not really feeling Ace's light weight, Clay Connery thought about his keel-boat as he and McAllen slogged along the river-bank towards distant Laredo.

He had become quite attached to that boat in the year he had operated it. Funny, he always thought of it as 'she'. The other rivermen had told him that all boats were female, whether they sailed rivers, lakes or the salty ocean. It had, at times, taken on a personal-ity of its own – or maybe he was just romancing things too much. But, no – in certain situations, caught in a river flood, a hammering deluge, unexpected rapids caused by some of the banks collapsing and narrow-ing the stream, at times like these when there was real danger, he had found himself actually talking to the boat as if it was a woman.

'Come on, Belle! Lift your skirts and dance your way through that white water! That's the gal! A turn to the right

now, sashay a lee-tle more left, a twirl and a jump – now we promenade into the quiet water. Ah! That's it, my beauty!'

He felt embarrassed just recalling such times, but although Ruben and McAllen had heard him on occasion they hadn't joshed him about it, or even looked at him queer. He had heard McAllen talking to the boat, too – mostly cussing and kicking the gunwales, but nonetheless making his contact with the vessel. Ruben, he'd seen murmuring quietly up in the bows at times and then his big hands would rub the gunwale in lingering caresses.

These were both men of the sea who had joined him and if it was good enough for them to commune with the *Belle*, then he reckoned it was OK for him, too.

Strange, when he had first come by the boat he had wanted to sell it, get a good price and then return to the hard-rock ranch he was trying to run back in Arizona.

The way he had come by the *Belle* still astounded him. He had trail-bossed a herd of longhorns up from Waco to Abilene, Kansas, leaving his dusty spread with its sod-walled cabin and falling-down corrals so as to get himself some money to renew these things, maybe enough to buy a starter herd.

A grubline rider who stopped by one night and actually gave Connery some hardtack, taking pity on him – told him about the cattlemen in Waco getting a big herd together and looking for an experienced trail boss.

'That's me,' Connery had told the rider. 'I been up the Chisholm, Goodnight-Loving and all the rest. Just got saddlesore-weary of the chore and figured

15

I'd try for a place of my own . . . ' He had smiled wryly and gestured towards the ragged piece of burlap that served as a door. 'Picked the wrong place – though it can be made good. *If* you've got the money to spend on it.'

'We-ell – you want to take the ride across to Waco, ask for Big Will Anniston.'

'Big Will?' Connery interrupted, looking excited. 'I've rid five thousand miles with that old wrangler. He's the one showed me the ropes. But, he must be nearing seventy by now. . . ?'

'Yeah – hasn't been trailin' cows for years. Married himself a gal about thirty years younger, got a slew of snotty-nosed kids and ain't set foot off his spread since he took his weddin' vows. That l'il gal sure tamed him down. . . .'

Anniston remembered Clay Connery all right, put him through his paces and gave him the job of trail-bossing the combined herds of the local ranchers to Abilene.

'Gotta be there by June 15th or we'll miss the first train north. Day late and your pay's cut in half.'

Connery smiled secretly: old Will Anniston hadn't changed all that much after all.

Well, they'd had a hell drive: flash floods, stampedes, Indians, rustlers – and the damn Kansans trying to turn them back, claiming the herd was bringing in Texas fever. Some knuckle skin was lost and some powder burned and a little blood spilled, but Connery brought the herd into Abilene – three days past the deadline. There was a week's wait for the next train.

16

Anniston was a man of his word: he cut Connery's pay by half but not the trail-hands' wages. Fact was, Connery finished up with only slightly more than if he had worked as a trail hand – without all the worry of being herd boss with its attendant responsibilities of finding water each day, negotiating with land owners so as to cross their pastures, making good fences broken or damaged by the cows and so on.

So he tried to build up that hard-earned money into a stake after a few drinks killed his misery and made him reckless. He sat in on a high-stakes poker game, local men and cattle buyers fogging up the private room with cigar smoke and the fumes of bonded liquor. Two dollars for every shot of that liquor it cost him – and the others. There were no favourites. So he didn't drink too much, while the others put it away in buckets.

He began to sober up and when he realized it he started to figure out the hands, what cards a player might need, judging by his discards just how strong a hand his opponent held. After a few mistakes that left him with a dwindling pile of cash in front of him, he suddenly got into the run of things and his luck turned.

He won hand after hand, lost a few, but not too expensively, then began to win again. And soon it became a contest between him and a man calling himself Blackjack Neale. Connery had no notion what the man did for a living, but he had wads of money, a seemingly endless thirst for brandy, and a recklessness such as he had never seen before.

The others tossed in their hands one by one and

the man next to him murmured a warning as he reached across for a vesta to light his cigarette.

'Jack's about to turn nasty. Does it every time. We try to dodge playin' with him if we can . . . cut out soon as you can.'

Connery appreciated the warning but there was a heap of money on that green baize cloth and he had visions of his broken-down ranch in Arizona – but with sprawling buildings and half-a-dozen riders, pastures green with water diverted from the creek, fat cows spread like a rusty red-and-white carpet all across his land clear back to the hills. . . .

He took a chance – and won.

He couldn't believe it. There was more than $3,000 in that pot and it was now his. Laughing as he pulled it across and scooped it into his hat, he said, 'Gents, I will buy you a round of drinks and then it's a bed in the best hotel in town for me! Maybe with a little company.' He winked. 'Just in case I feel like talking during the night!'

That got a half-hearted laugh and the drinks were readily accepted. But he noticed the locals were watching Neale warily. Blackjack, face bloated and his breath hissing through his nose, leaned forward, eyes narrowed.

'You ain't going no place with my money, feller – not without givin' me a chance to win it back, you ain't!'

Silence filled that smoke-fogged, stuffy room, dragged on a long minute. Then Connery looked across the table at Neale, saw the craziness in the man's eyes. He shook his head slowly. 'Taken me too

18

long to win it, friend. Sorry. I'm through – and I need this stake real bad.'

Chairs scraped as they were pushed back from the table, but the men didn't vacate the room: they stood around the wall, waiting to see the next development.

Neale scowled at Connery. 'You're just too damn lucky, mister!'

Connery held up a hand quickly. 'Leave it right there, Neale – I won't take offence at that. But it'll be best all round if you don't take it any further.'

Two men left the room in a hurry. The other three stood very still, eyes moving from Neale to Connery. Blackjack had risen slightly from his chair but Connery hadn't moved position, just watched the man with hard, wary eyes. Something Neale saw made him sit down slowly. Suddenly he grinned, then pulled out his jacket front quickly and reached inside.

There was a gasp as Connery suddenly held a cocked six-gun pointing at the loser. Neale's face popped sweat and he swallowed, slowly eased his hand out – showing that he was only reaching for a wallet, now grasped in trembling fingers.

Every man there knew that Connery could have killed Neale if he'd wanted to.

'One bet,' croaked Neale. 'Just one chance for me to get some of that money back – no! You put up *all* of it.'

'I don't want any kind of a bet, mister,' Connery told him, holstering the gun slowly. 'I told you that. Anyway, you've got no money, you said.'

Neale smiled and drew a paper from his wallet and dropped it on the table. 'The *Little Whore* – best keel-boat ever to kiss water! Worth all of three thousand as you'll see by that bill of sale. See? Right here. I put that up agin your cash. One draw: high card wins.'

'That's a loco move, my friend,' Connery said but although Neale's smile tightened it didn't fade right away.

'Loco or not, that's the deal – you gonna take it?'

'About the last thing in this world I've got a use for is a keelboat, Jack.' Connery shook his head, went on putting away his winnings. 'I live in the desert in Arizona!'

Neale's hand shot out, grabbed his wrist. Their gazes met and the three other card players moved back a step. Neale's teeth bared.

'Somebody get a new deck,' he said quietly. 'This feller's gonna play high-card draw with me. It's only right to gimme a chance to win back my *dinero*.'

'You had plenty of chances, mister.'

Connery twisted free and stood back. They could almost see it pass through his mind: kill this stupid son of a bitch and get out of here. Or . . .

'OK – bring on a new deck,' Connery said abruptly, startling everyone. He didn't know what made him change his mind but Neale's smile warmed as he dropped into his chair.

'*Now* someone fetch a new deck!! he gritted.

One of the men went to fetch a sealed deck of cards. Connery studied the sweating Neale. 'Why would a man who's already lost so much, playing cards so damn reckless the way you do, make a stupid

20

bet that'll ruin him if he loses?'

Neale laughed. 'I ain't gonna lose, friend! I'm gonna be rich again!' He struck his chest. 'Feel it right in here! That's why I just can't walk away – I gotta *try*!'

Connery grunted, picking up the papers, reading about the keelboat, which seemed to be only a few months old and, sure enough, was called *Little Whore*. Thirty feet long, square sail, deckhouse, cargo hold, double keel for river work, ironwood mast and tiller, hull and ribs built of oak, drawing only a couple of feet.

'How about when she's loaded?' Connery asked, surprised that he could come up with a reasonable sounding query for he knew nothing at all about boats of any kind.

'Depends on how much is in the hold and how heavy,' Neale answered, looking around anxiously, impatiently waiting for the new cards. 'She'll navigate most rivers from the Missouri to the Rio. . . .'

'You been working it?'

'Not me – Brother Deke has . . . no need to look like that. I own it. Deke just works for shares   Ah! At last!'

The new deck was unwrapped by the man who brought it in and, at a nod from Connery, shuffled it well, several times, until Neale shouted for him to put the goddamn pack down on the goddamn table and let him get on with the goddamn draw! Connery was tense but tried not to show it. He had had a long run of luck and felt it was still working for him – though what he would do with a boat, the Good Lord only knew. He would sell it, maybe, and have enough for a really good ranch. . . . Yeah! That would be best.

And if he lost?

'King of spades!' crowed Neale suddenly, letting out a warwhoop like a drunken Comanche, waving a card around. 'See if you can beat that, Connery!'

Connery hadn't been aware the man was making his draw, refused an offer to have the deck shuffled again, and drew his own card without hesitation.

He looked across at Neale who was mopping his damp face with a kerchief now, nostrils pinched, bloated cheeks looking sunken, his breathing ragged.

'Come *on*, damn you! Show your card!'

The trail boss slowly turned over the card on the green baize, face up.

Ace of clubs.

There was a sigh from the gamblers and Neale slumped in his chair, face drained of blood, staring at the card bitterly. Then he snapped his head up, forcing a smile. 'Well, I reckon you take first draw.' He glanced around as everyone stared at him uncomprehendingly.'Well, that's what this was for. I just cut the deck to take a card to see who has first draw – that's the rules. Right?'

'I must've gotten more trail dust in my ears than I thought,' Connery said slowly, his gaze pinning Neale in his chair like twin arrows. 'I never heard you say anything about them rules.'

Neale made himself look bewildered. 'But – it's taken for granted! Shuffle the deck, cut it to see who draws first. . . .'

'You didn't cut, Jack,' said Connery. 'You drew

your card, told me to beat your king – which I did, with my ace. Which makes me the winner.'

Connery picked up the boat papers again and Neale jumped up, eyes wild. 'No! That was just to decide who draws the cards first. We have the real draw now!' He looked around at the three gamblers against the wall. 'You men know that!'

They all shook their heads slowly, looking tensed, and the middle man said, 'You changed the rules because his card beat yours, Jack. You can't do that – you lost. Fair and square.'

'By hell! I knew it! It was all a set-up! You sons of bitches set out to fleece me rotten right from the start. . . .'

Neale was waving his arms about, taking jerky steps, making the gamblers move uneasily. But he used the motions to cover his draw – not a card this time, but a gun from a shoulder holster. One of the gamblers dropped, shouting a warning, and the others ran for the door.

Jack heaved the table into Connery and sent him sprawling and wrenched a spilled chair aside shooting at the trail man. Connery rolled as splinters sprayed his face and he triggered his Colt, rising on one elbow. The bullet took Neale in the middle of the chest and the man slumped, taking his time, his smoking gun falling from his grip, blood spreading across his shirt front and vest. He jarred to his knees and spread out on his side, twitching twice.

The room filled with people from the saloon bar and the law arrived in a few minutes, a tough marshal and two deputies.

There were plenty of witnesses, each in good standing locally, to back Connery's story.

He rode out the same night, pockets bulging, heading for Las Cruces, New Mexico, where the keelboat was said to be working the rivers under the captaincy of Deke Neale.

What Connery found was that Deke had been killed in an argument over a hand of cards – Must run in the family! thought Connery – and the boat was half-sunk on a mudbank, used by birds and a couple of drunks as a home. No one could remember the last time it had carried a real cargo.

Connery had to salvage it if he was going to sell it and it took money to do that. He had to hire men to clean it up, a boat builder to repair splintered hull planks, a sailmaker, and a man to cut and trim a new mast. He did what he could himself to help, but he found his stake had dwindled alarmingly by the time he had finished – then learned that no one was interested in keelboats these days, not in the south, leastways. Paddle-wheelers were all the go and Richard King of the King Ranch was the man who had the monopoly of river trade on the Rio with a fleet of twenty steamboats.

The big man himself happened to be in El Paso so Connery rode on down, finally got to see him and tried to sell him the keelboat, now renamed the *Rio Belle*.

King was a sober man, not given to much laughter, but he laughed at Connery.

'My friend, keelboats aren't suitable for the Rio Grande and still you try to sell one to *me*!' Two of

King's sidekicks moved in on Connery but the big man held up a hand and nodded. 'Let him talk.'

'Just thought you might have some use for a smaller boat, Mr King, taking fast messages between your steamers or something. I don't know anything about the river trade. I'm trying to get money to build up my spread in Arizona.'

King studied him, frowning a little. 'I think I believe you, Connery. Tell you what, you want to work that keelboat on the Rio, you go right ahead – but' – he smiled thinly – 'on the Mexican side only. The American side is mine. You stay clear of it. If you can make a few bucks carrying the trash the Mexes want to ship out, then good luck to you. Just don't say I didn't warn you that you'll go bust in less than a month.'

King's retinue were grinning, highly amused. Connery felt himself tightening up under the mocking stares.

'All right, Mr King – I'll even thank you for what you obviously see as your generosity. But, I'll be still sailing the *Rio Belle* on this river, and making a profit, in a year's time.' He cursed inwardly for making such a boast

'Connery, I've got a queer feeling about you. I think you just might make a go of it – in a limited way. You won't ever be any kind of a risk to my trade, but I can admire a man with guts. Just be sure you keep to your side of the river.'

Connery tried, after finding a couple of stranded seaman – McAllen and Ruben – who showed him how to handle a boat, taught him how to read the river's currents and moods. The trading side of it he picked up easily enough, having done a slew of cattle buying over the years.

So he nudged into the river trade, struggling, losing money through inexperience, but learning as he went, using his mistakes to set him on the right path.

Then the vultures swooped, making ridiculous offers for the boat. *Maybe they saw potential he couldn't.* The thought made him dig in his heels and once again he cursed his innate stubbornness. There was even an offer from a man who had been in the poker game in Abilene. Connery didn't remember his name, only the square face and the tough manner. Maybe Kelly? Or Kiley. . . ? Didn't matter. He wasn't selling.

'Your run of luck ended at that card table in Abilene, mister. Cut your losses and go back to your cows is my advice.'

'Don't have enough to do that – and your offer for the boat won't improve things. I'll hold on a bit longer.'

The man didn't like that, had been sure of success.

'Damn you, my price is fair!'

Connery gave him his hard stare. 'Never did like to be crowded.'

'Listen, maybe you could lose that boat – you dunno the river, you could hit a rock. Fires start easy on boats with all that tar and hemp around. . . .'

'I'd go a'hunting if *my* boat caught fire,' Connery told him, and watched the blood drain from the man's face.

26

'Damn you, Connery! I've got a chance to make a killin' with a boat like you've got . . . it's the only one on the Rio!'

'Then I could charge double what you're offering – I reckon we're all through talking.'

There was a veiled challenge in that and for a moment he thought the man was going to accept, but then he spun on his heel and shouldered through the watching men, muttering, square face flushed with humiliation. A man he considered no more than a river rat had sent him packing. But he had been there when Blackjack had been shot down and he wasn't about to test his gun speed against Connery. . . .

Connery swore silently: that damn stubbornness again had put him on a spot . . . now he had to work the river.

But suddenly he began to show a profit, small at first, then more and more. Still nothing like even one of King's paddle-wheeler's made, but it was a start.

He had long ago pushed his plans about the Arizona spread aside but in the back of his mind now he knew he would one day return to cattle ranching It was in his blood.

Maybe this time he would go back with a bankroll.

CHAPTER 3

FORBIDDEN CARGO

It was a rainy day for the funeral and only Connery, Ruben and McAllen attended, with a couple of the undertaker's helpers and the grave digger.

By this time, Connery knew he didn't have much money to play with, having seen the Texas National Bank branch on South-west Republic Street. But he ordered a headstone for Ace, had it engraved simply:

'Ace' – By name and by nature.
His shipmates of the
Rio Belle

'Pretty good gravestone for a runaway kid who never even told us his second name,' opined McAllen, sourly.

'Maybe I'll do as much for you when the time comes, Mac,' Connery told him shortly, and McAllen sneered a little but shook his head slowly.

'You're a soft touch, Skipper.'

All Ruben said was, 'Fine gesture, Cap. Real fine.'

Connery had hired men to unload the *Rio Belle* and he knew now she was past salvaging. Too much damage under the waterline and the mast had sprung several ribs and shattered part of the deck.

'Nothing to do but write it off,' Connery decided and the others agreed. 'We'll save what we can of the cargo, sort it out, ship on the good stuff by wagon and compensate the owners of whatever's missing from the manifest.'

'You'll be broke,' McAllen pointed out unnecessarily. 'There gonna be enough to pay me and Rube?'

'Not in advance – I'll pay you when I get paid for delivery.'

McAllen spat but Ruben merely nodded. Connery left them to supervise the unloading and salvaging, went to see a man named Vincenz, a shipping agent he had used previously on a few occasions.

Vinnie Vincenz was mostly Mexican – the rest was anyone's guess, but some said there was a little Chinese, some German and even a smattering of South Sea Islander. He was a solidly built, medium-tall man with a flourishing black moustache and a small triangle of beard under his lower lip. He smiled a lot and spoke American with a pleasant accent.

He greeted Connery effusively, shaking his hand, leading him across his small office to a chair in front of his desk. He poured two whiskies from a bottle he had to break the seal on first.

That should have warned Connery – Vinnie never

gave anyone his 'special' treatment unless he was planning on getting plenty in return. But they drank a silent toast, and Vinnie went back behind his cluttered desk.

'I hear of your misfortune, Captain. It sadden me, because I know you have put much effort and money into your boat – she is finish, I am told.'

'Yeah, Vinnie – at least I'm pretty sure she is. But after we off-load I'll drag her up on the bank and make sure. Might be able to do a few repairs to keep her going a little longer.'

Vinnie's black hair glinted in a stray shaft of sunlight that had found a way through the dusty window pane behind his desk. He shrugged. 'Big job, Captain. Very expensive, work on boats. But what can I do to help?'

'Well, I'll need to sort out whatever cargo we can salvage, then ship it on to Brownsville and Matamoros. I'll need a couple of wagons. Can you arrange them? On hire, of course.'

'*Sí*, naturally, Captain – I know of two Conestoga wagons that should be available, the original Pennsylvania type, larger than the immigrant prairie wagons that so many people use now. . . . You would wish to make the sides higher, perhaps? Carry more freight?'

'Well, I dunno just yet, but I'd like the option.'

Vinnie made notes. 'And it will be cheaper for you and perhaps even faster if you use oxen instead of mules or horses – both of which are very expensive to hire. Such hard work, drawing a freight wagon, Captain.'

Connery frowned. 'Never driven an ox-team.'

'*Sencillo, Capitano! Muy sencillo!*'

Connery still seemed unsure despite the agent's assurance that it was a simple matter.

'There are no reins, Captain. You use a whip, walk at the front beside the leader – I believe I can give you a man. . . .' He turned to a small book, opened it and leafed through a couple of pages before nodding. 'Yes – Latigo. A good man, reliable, honest.'

Connery let that last go – not too many of Vinnie's men could be classed as honest. The man was a rogue and was much more at ease employing other rogues. But Connery appreciated the offer and accepted with thanks.

'There will be no charge, Captain. Latigo can handle some business for me in Brownsville. It will all work out very well.' He started to close the book, then looked up suddenly. 'Er – if there should be room, Captain, you would like, perhaps, a small cargo to deliver? It will help offset your not inconsiderable expenses. . . ?'

Connery had gone very still. He rolled and lit a cigarette, watching Vinnie, the man's smile slowly fading and his fingers fidgeting with a pencil until it broke.

'I've carried cargo for you before, Vinnie.'

'Of course, Captain! And most successfully, too. That is why I make you this offer.'

Connery had an idea what kind of cargo it would be – not specifically, but in general. Sure to be something that the Customs wouldn't like to pass across the border without payment of duty. He had know-ingly carried such items a couple of times when money was short. Vinnie had arranged things well and there had been no trouble, but he had made it clear after the second time – when things had almost gone wrong – that it would be the last time.

Now – well, he certainly needed every cent he could lay hands to, but if anything did go wrong it would only add to the disaster that had already befallen him.

At the same time, he didn't want Vinnie to with-draw all the offered help. Although the agent hadn't said as much, Connery knew it was inferred: *You help me, I help you.*

'Tell you what, Vinnie, let's leave things until I see how much freight I can rescue from the *Belle*. If there's room left in the wagons after we load, maybe we can make some arrangements.'

He could see by Vinnie's face that it was not to his liking. The agent lowered his voice, glanced at the closed door and leaned forward across the desk. 'Captain, it was indeed fortuitous that your – calamity – occurred when it did. For me, I mean, because it happens that I have a special shipment that must go as soon as possible. You are popular along the river, Captain, both sides. The Customs will be sympathetic because of your troubles. They will not add to your travail by making you off-load everything and may well simply wave you through—'

'You cunning little so-and-so, Vinnie!' Connery said, with some amusement. 'That scrambled brain of yours must've worked overtime last night as soon as you heard the *Belle* was stranded. You knew I'd have to come to you for wagons. But, if you're worried about passing this shipment through Customs, you're falling down on the job, Vinnie. Usually you have such things well arranged in advance.'

Vinnie sat back, trying to keep his smile going, but it was shrinking by the minute. He spread his hands. 'We all have our emergencies, Captain! This is a perfect opportunity for us to help each other. And you will profit, I assure you.'

Connery was sober now. 'You still mixed up with those Mexican radicals? You had a brother-in-law who was organizing some sort of resistance move, didn't you?'

'Captain!' Vinnie looked hurt and spread his hands again. 'But I am no longer married to that *bruja*, his sister!'

'She might be a witch, Vinnie, and you might *not* be married to her now, but you and her brother – Fredrico, isn't it? – had a profitable little business going. You wouldn't allow a divorce to interfere with that.' Connery held up a hand as Vinnie started to protest. 'I know you that well, Vinnie. Told you last time when they came close to finding those guns that I wanted no more forbidden cargoes.'

'Captain, I swear – on the grave of my mother – that these are not guns! Why, I can show you the boxes.' He made dimensions in the air with his hands. 'No bigger than this.'

'A box that size could hold a dozen pistols.'

'No, no! I tell you on my honour, Captain, no guns!'

Connery stood abruptly. 'Well, just let's leave things as they are, Vinnie. I appreciate your help. Will you arrange for the wagons and send one out to where the wreck is and we'll bring in the cargo as we salvage it?'

'And if there is room, you will take my special packages?'

'Let's wait and see how much room we have – OK?'

Vinnie shrugged helplessly and his smile was almost non-existent as he showed Connery to the door.

It took most of the day to unload the *Belle*, the salvaged cargo spread out along the banks. The casks and most of the boxes were all right, unaffected by the water, only two boxes had damaged corners. Some bales of goat and deer skins would have to be opened, the contents spread out to dry. Paper-wrapped parcels would have to be examined individually before a decision could be reached about their contents. Ruben, that first afternoon, had done an excellent job of saving the timber shipment from being washed away down-river, never to be seen again. Only a dozen or so lengths were lost, and, surprisingly, the bottled goods had not been entirely destroyed. Connery had expected ninety per cent of them to be shattered, but there was still more than fifty per cent intact, thanks to them having been stowed amongst the bales. Handtooled leather work did not suffer as much as expected either, thanks to good packing and the fact that each and every item had been well rubbed with neat's-foot oil or beeswax.

Most fabric goods, hand-sewn tablecloths, doilies and table napkins would have to be dried out before they could be assessed.

Still, he knew there would be quite a big loss and he would have to go into debt to compensate the poor Mexicans who had shipped them . . . they were mostly peasants who had used the *Rio Belle*. Recompense for loss had been one of the conditions of carrying such cargo and he had agreed to it so he would have to hold up his end of the bargain.

But he was pleasantly surprised to find that the hull of the *Belle* wasn't as badly damaged as they had first thought. They used some of the oxen that Vinnie had sent with the wagon to carry the salvaged goods back to town to haul the hulk close inshore, free of the sand bars and the current.

'A good carpenter might repair that,' Mac said, looking at the damaged keelboat. 'Not easy, but could be done.'

'Mast'll be the problem – and the deck's sprung pretty bad,' allowed Ruben.

'Maybe we could rip up the deck, make it an open hold, just cover the load with tarps,' suggested Connery and there was a discussion about it without any real decision being arrived at.

But it was a possibility to give some thought to. . . .

Vinnie's wagon had a crew of three Mexicans bossed by a big white man named Brock. He was hard on the Mexicans but they obeyed in sullen silence and worked well at loading the casks and undamaged boxes on to the wagon. It was almost dark then and Brock swaggered across to where

Connery was marking off his cargo manifest.

'Figured we might's well take that undamaged stuff back to the store shed when we go back to town.'

Connery glanced up, looked past Brock's beefy shoulder to where the Mexicans were loading the small Studebaker wagon. 'Good idea – thanks. Been a long day.'

'Well, Vinnie'll have your Conestogas back there so we can start loadin'. Save you some time.'

Connery studied the big man. Brock was about six feet two, a couple of inches taller than Connery, wider in the chest and shoulders, too. He had long, wheat-coloured hair showing thickly beneath his hat, a sparse blond moustache along the upper lip of a hard mouth. There were thin scars above the mocking blue eyes and the nose was not quite as straight as it should be. Connery dropped his eyes to the man's hands. Big, large knuckles with scars, thick wrists. A powerful man who had done a lot of fighting.

And he didn't seem the type to be as obliging as he was acting. He was new since Connery had last dealt with Vincenz, but he knew he had to be the agent's troubleshooter.

'Vinnie giving me the royal treatment, is he?'

Brock shrugged. 'I just do what I'm told. I was you, I'd be glad of the extra help.'

He started to swing away and Connery said, 'Buy you a drink if I see you in town.'

He thought Brock grunted but there was no other acknowledgement.

They had lanterns burning before they were

through. Connery had sent the men Vinnie had loaned him for the salvage work back to town with a dollar apiece. That left himself, McAllen and Ruben.

'C'mon – I'll buy you supper and couple of drinks,' Connery offered. 'I've seen the banker and he's advanced me some cash. Not much, but something to work with.'

'Gimme some in hand,' McAllen said. 'I spotted a fine little Mex filly flashin' her teeth and a couple other interestin' things at me standin' outside a place called Babylon.' He paused to wink. 'I ain't a Bible man but I know enough to figure I could have a fine time there.'

'Sure you ain't thinkin' of Sodom and Gomorrah?' asked Ruben.

'Well, I could be thinkin' along them lines!'

Connery smiled slowly. 'If that's what you want, Mac – but we start early tomorrow.' He handed McAllen some coins, looked quizzically at Ruben who hesitated, then put out his hand, too.

'I better go keep an eye on him.' he said, deadpan.

Laughing, muscles aching, they went back to town and Connery bought a couple of rounds of drinks before Ruben and McAllen went in search of Babylon.

Connery had a meal, bought himself a decent shirt and some tobacco and strolled around town. He stopped at a gunsmith's to admire a double-action Smith & Wesson pistol, when he caught a reflection of light in the window glass at the far end. The shop was opposite Vinnie's warehouse and the big, long building was in darkness, except for a small light somewhere deep inside, glinting through a gap in the warped boards. Connery frowned, seeing the light disappear and then reappear – as if someone had walked between it and the crack in the wall planks.

Idly curious, he strolled through the considerable night traffic of Laredo's main drag and walked through the weeds of the lot where the storehouse stood, back from the street front, backing on to the river. He put an eye to the large gap in the warped boards and worked his head around so he could see properly. He took off his hat and that allowed him to get his face closer and he saw men moving around in there – loading casks and boxes on to a big, heavy, high-sided Conestoga wagon, one he was hiring from Vinnie Vincenz.

Looked like Brock was as good as his word.

He found a small door further along, eased it open and stepped inside to the smells of dust, burlap and oil, herbs and horses and dung. He stood in some of the latter and swore as he scraped it off his boot.

The men working on the wagon heard him and light from the lanterns they were working by glinted off gunmetal as he heard a rifle lever work swiftly.

'Who's that?' barked a deep voice, that he recognized as belonging to Brock.

'Connery.' He started forward into the circle of light, saw the sweating Mexicans, two lumbering a big cask towards the tailgate, two others carrying a small pine box each.

No one said anything as he walked around the rear of the big wagon and looked inside. The casks and some bales had been stowed neatly enough, but there was a gap left in the middle. There were three pine boxes just like the ones the Mexicans now held already in place.

Connery looked at Brock whose cold blue eyes didn't waver. 'What the hell d'you think you're doing?'

'Savin' you and your men some time tomorrow – what's it look like?'

'It looks like you're not only loading my cargo, but you're using it to hide those boxes in the middle of it.'

Brock said nothing, face impassive. The Mexicans were still a frozen tableau.

Connery gestured to one of the men holding the boxes. 'Open that up.'

The man looked afraid, rolled his eyes towards Brock. The boss man allowed the rifle barrel to swing around casually in Connery's direction.

'Can't do that.'

'Why not?'

'Take a look – Customs wire.'

Connery had already noticed. 'It's wire, but doesn't look like Customs wire to me – no seals for a start. I want to see what's in there.'

'Just gears and cotter pins, with tools to fit 'em in some kinda machinery on the railroad they're building in the Hermoso Valley up to Brownsville. See the brand? An American company. You gotta recognize that name.'

Connery stared at him levelly. 'Anyone could stencil that on.'

'What was that?' Brock asked quietly, and the Mexicans set down the boxes on top of the casks. They faded back into the shadows as the two men faced each other.

'There might be machine parts in there, but what else is with 'em? What's hidden underneath?'

'You ain't callin' me a liar, are you, Connery?'

'No – I'll give you the benefit of the doubt. I'd say you're just not telling me everything; likely just repeating what Vinnie told you to.'

'Then that ought to be good enough.'

'Not by a damn sight.'

Brock nodded very gently. 'Uh-huh – heard about you, Connery. Fast with a gun, they say. Good with your fists. True?'

Connery smiled crookedly, set his parcel down on the wagon tailgate. 'I've a notion you're itching to find out.'

Brock grinned – then lunged forward and jabbed the rifle muzzle into Connery's midriff, brought the butt around smartly as Connery doubled up.

The brass shoulder piece skidded along the side of Connery's head, knocking his hat off – and dropping the man to his knees, swaying, only semi-conscious.

Brock stepped in and brought up his knee into Connery's face. The keelboat man stretched out on the straw-littered ground, nose spurting blood. Brock rested the rifle across one of the casks, rubbed his hands together and moved in, drawing back his right boot.

Instinct saved the riverboat man: head throbbing, senses swimming, he knew the danger he was in lying down here on the floor and he rolled away from the kick, vaguely hearing Brock's curse as the man stumbled off balance.

By then Connery had his six-gun out and the hammer cocked with a cold sound. He tried to speak but his tongue was too thick in his mouth.

Actions speak louder than words, he thought – and swung the gun barrel hard and brutally across Brock's shins. The man howled and danced, reaching down for his throbbing leg. Connery thrust to one knee and slammed the gun barrel across the side of Brock's head.

The freight-man fell to hands and knees. Connery crawled across to him, reared up and whipped the gun barrel back and forth across the big, heavy face.

Brock's head jerked on his shoulders, first to the left, then to the right. The gun barrel whipped again and blood streaked the torn and battered face as Brock sighed harshly and collapsed, arms sliding out from under him.

Connery swayed, blinking hard, shaking his head, tasting blood from his squashed nostrils.

He looked around and for the first time saw the narrow set of stairs leading above to a small room where a light glowed. Gun at the ready, he moved towards it, surging anger giving him strength and purpose.

CHAPTER 4

RIVER TRAIL

The stairs were narrow but not steep and Connery moved quietly, beginning to remember now.

He hadn't been in this part of the warehouse before, but Vinnie had told him once about the 'special office' he had had built in the large building. He was still married to the woman he called 'the witch' at the time but this was his trysting place, where he could meet and romance the women he charmed into coming here.

So, Connery was not too surprised when he opened the door quietly and in the light of several burning candles, and an atmosphere thick with the sweetish, lingering smell of the drug weed *hachis*, saw the man and woman on the bed.

Actually, the woman was beside the bed, bending over the man, her naked, oiled back to Connery, buttocks glinting in the flickering light. Dark hair spilled across the side of her face and she appeared to be undressing the squirming Vinnie with her teeth. She was peeling off his shirt and it came free even as Connery watched, and then she bent lower and her teeth worked at the waistband of his trousers.

Connery shook himself and stepped forward. She must have heard him, started to turn quickly, but he grabbed some of that swinging, raven hair and pulled her away roughly. She cried out as she stumbled back and he saw she was young, probably not yet even twenty years old.

Vinnie's eyes were wide and although he was still under the influence of the *hachis*, he turned and groped wildly under his pillow. Connery stepped over the writhing girl as she struggled to get to her feet, handicapped by the heavy oiling of her flesh. He cuffed Vinnie across the ear, twisted fingers in the man's hair and yanked his head back savagely. Vinnie moaned and clawed at the hair, dropping the gun he had dragged out from beneath the pillow. The whites of his eyes were showing, but he recognized Connery as the man shook him violently. The girl gave another small cry and swept up a bundled skirt and blouse and dived out the doorway.

'Captain!' Vinnie gasped, a nervous, jumpy smile writhing across his trembling lips.

'You slimy worm, Vinnie! I told you I would take it over only *if* there was enough room to carry any special goods!'

'But there was room, Captain! Brock told me so! We – we were just saving you time. . . !'

Connery shook him roughly, hearing the man's

teeth clack together as his head rocked on his shoulders. 'Save me time? Likely I'd end up *doing* time if I'd taken those boxes over the border without even knowing I had 'em!'

Vinnie was off the bed now, down on his knees, the fingers of Connery's left hand locked in his hair. 'Captain, I meant well!'

'You meant well – for yourself! Damnit, Vinnie, I likely would've taken whatever contraband is in those boxes, but not now. We talk *deals*. You don't try to shove your damn stuff down my throat without even asking permission!'

'I-I apologize, Captain! Of course, it was stupid of me, I should have talked with you first! But there are only five boxes, such small ones, so easily hidden by your cargo. . . .'

'I don't do business that way, Vinnie, and you know it – and I'm gonna make sure, damn sure, you don't forget it!'

He dragged the now screaming Vincenz to the door, kicked it open, heaved him out on to the tiny landing and threw him down the stairs. The girl was just tying her skirt's waistband as her lover came tumbling and somersaulting down, trying to scream, but the sounds smashed back into his throat by his jarring on the stairs. She took one look at the wild-eyed, bloody-faced Connery as he came down stiffly, gun in hand, and ran towards the street door. She left it open after she had dived through.

Vinnie was moaning, almost unconscious, when Connery reached his huddled body at the foot to the stairs. Brock was still out of it and looked a mess, his face like raw meat.

Connery ripped off his old stained and torn work shirt, wiped his bloody nose and flung the garment into a dark corner. He tore open the wrapping on his new shirt, put it on and went out into the night.

He and McAllen and Ruben had decided they would sleep on the river-bank just along from the pier to save money and he made his way there, grunted as he sat down in the dewy grass. He took off his hat to use as a pillow, and stretched out, holding his sixgun in his hand.

Long hours of work, the beating at Brock's hands, plus the liquor helped him slide easily into a deep sleep.

It was still dark when rough hands shook his shoulder and he automatically rolled away, bringing the Colt around, thumb searching for the hammer spur.

'Cap! Cap! Wake up, man!'

It was Ruben's voice and Connery's sleep-fogged eyes cleared as he rubbed a hand across them. He glimpsed Rubin kneeling beside him, saw another figure standing, swaying, by some bushes, hearing a sound of hissing water that he knew did not come from the river.

McAllen relieving his bladder, he thought, raised his gaze to Ruben again and then paused, moving his head to the left, looking upstream.

Something had caught his eye in that direction, a kind of flickering, reflected from the river in bursts of amber and crimson.

'Fire, Cap!' Ruben said, even as his senses registered the fact. 'Comin' from where we left the boat. . . .'

Connery started to his feet and Ruben took his arm, helping him up. 'Figured we'd find you sleepin' here,' Ruben explained, steadying his captain. 'Mac's a little worse for his visit to Babylon and I had to leave me a snake-clingin' honey to make sure he got back safe. Looks bad, Cap.'

'Mac, you with us?' Connery was awake now, his face hurting, but he holstered the gun, grabbed McAllen's arm. 'Let's go. . . .'

The town was still alive with noise and drunks and shrill women and there were plenty of horses tied up at the hitching racks. Connery and his friends borrowed a mount each from outside Babylon and rode out along the Rio towards the fire.

There was only a pile of collapsed, blackened timber, still glowing and flickering here and there, when they arrived. What had been left of the *Rio Belle* was now nothing more than charred planks.

And a powerful smell of coal oil.

In amongst the smouldering wood they saw broken jars and lots of blackened glass. 'Son of a bitch must've used about three or four gallons to make sure she went up fast,' Connery allowed, fingering a piece of jagged jar neck.

'Hell,' McAllen said, swaying as he stared. 'Now that's gonna take a mighty good carpenter to put right!' He slurred his words and started to laugh.

Ruben shook him but McAllen didn't stop laughing, stumbled and sat down on the grass, shaking with his mirth.

'Guess that finishes it, Cap,' Ruben said quietly.

Connery nodded, face grim in the crimson glow. He gestured to where they had left some of the water-damaged goods to dry out a little overnight. 'Never touched anything else – just fired the *Belle*. That ought to tell us something.'

Ruben turned liquour-reddened eyes to Connery. 'Reckon you'll have a time provin' anythin', Cap'n.'

Connery nodded. 'I reckon so, too, but I *know*. . . . Well, it's done now. Thing is to get them wagons started towards Brownsville. The people I'm interested in will still be here when we get back.'

Ruben nodded. McAllen had toppled over on to his side and was snoring happily.

Connery was up early, bathed in the river, his nose swollen and red, an inflamed-looking knot on his forehead. But when he went to Vinnie's warehouse, he figured he didn't look too bad compared to Brock.

A gun-whipping leaves unmistakable signs and Brock's face was swollen and misshapen, red-and-purple-and-blue welts on either side of his battered nose. His eyes were blackened and his mouth puffy under the wispy blond moustache. He scowled at Connery when he came in, a badly hungover McAllen stumbling along reluctantly. Ruben was there, too, as bright as if he had retired just after sundown last night without tasting either red eye or women, and slept the sleep of the just.

Brock stood squarely in front of Connery. 'You and me – no one does what you did to me and keeps walkin' around.'

Connery looked more closely at the man now. His eyebrows and the front of his pale hair seemed strange somehow – then he saw what it was: parts of them were now brown or black, the ends of individual hairs curled. Connery had seen scorch marks before many times.

'That coal oil go up with a rush?' he asked levelly and Brock frowned, stepped back a pace. He ran a tongue over his lips, scrubbed at his jaw. And Connery saw the blisters on the back of the big hand. He stepped around the puzzled freighter to some shelves where there stood stone jars and half-gallon bottles labelled Coal Oil. Hard eyes swivelled to the tensed Brock.

'Few empty spaces among the bottles and jars. . . .'

'Yeah? Must've been sold or shipped out with an order.'

'Or taken out to the *Rio Belle*, used to saturate the timbers and then a match tossed in. All that oil would go with a flash and a man'd have to be mighty quick to step back.' Connery touched his eyebrows. 'Looks like you weren't quick enough, Brock.'

'What? You sayin' I fired your damned boat? You're a goddamn liar if you are!'

Ruben and McAllen moved swiftly to one side and the Mexican workers within hearing quit whatever jobs they were doing and hurried back into the deep shadows of the warehouse, well clear of the *gringos*.

Connery smiled bleakly. 'I don't let any man call me a liar, Brock.'

'Well? What you aim to do about it?' Brock was already drawing his gun as he spoke, moving a step to one side, crouching as his Colt snapped into line.

His mouth sagged open an instant before the sixgun that had appeared in Connery's hand blazed. Brock was flung backwards violently by the strike of the bullet, his own Colt firing at an angle, the slug shattering one of the coal oil jars. Brock sobbed as he dropped to his knees, left hand pressed into the bleeding wound in his side. Connery stepped up alongside and kicked the smoking pistol from Brock's right hand. The freighter looked up with wide, apprehensive eyes as Connery placed a boot against his chest and slammed him brutally to the ground. Brock grunted, on the verge of passing out. Connery leaned down to him.

'See me again when I get back and we'll finish this – I'm in kind of a hurry right now,' Connery told him coldly, and there was something in his eyes that sent a massive bolt of fear through Brock just before he plunged into unconsciousness.

Vinnie's voice, shaking a little, spoke from his office doorway. 'Is he – dead, Captain?'

'He'll live – but you'd best get him to a doctor, one that won't call that damn Marshal, if you know one.'

Vinnie nodded, called two Mexicans and spoke rapidly to them in Spanish. As they lifted the unconscious and bleeding Brock, Connery turned to Ruben and McAllen. 'Boys, stay here and keep an eye on things – you know what I mean.'

Ruben and McAllen went to supervise the loading of the huge wagons, made to the original design developed by Pennsylvanian farmers and freighters, built of heavy, solid timbers. Only later did they cut down the size and weight to something more manageable for the inexperienced migrants on their treks west to the Promised Land. The migrant version was shorter, narrower, the sides lower. These big wagons that Vinnie had procured would carry twice as much. 'Your quarrel was only with Brock I hope,' Vinnie said.

'Let's go talk about it – you reckon those shots would've been heard outside here?'

'I think not, Captain,' Vinnie said, slowly, wary of this man who had just out-shot his hired gunfighter.

Vinnie had one arm in a sling. His mouth was swollen and there was a gap in his weak smile now as he led Connery into his office, leaning heavily on a stick. His face was bruised, his every movement stiff and obviously took much effort. 'You were very hard on me last night, Captain – I think it will be a long time before I forgive you entirely.'

'Well, get to work on it – unless you already started last night.'

Vinnie frowned and it was clear to Connery that the man didn't know what he was getting at. 'The special boxes have been unloaded from your wagon, Captain. You may check the loading of your goods if you wish.'

'My men are already doing that. You know anything about my boat being burned last night?'

Connery was puzzled because once again Vinnie's shock seemed genuine. Watching the agent closely, he told him about the fire. Vinnie had paled, already nervous over the shooting in his warehouse. Now he knew he was suspected of the arson, but he held out his good hand imploringly, trying to act at his ease.

'So that was your trouble with Brock! But, Captain, it was not me! I know nothing about it. I swear on my mother's grave . . . I . . .'

'All right, Vinnie. That poor old mother of yours! Wouldn't surprise me none if she was still alive and kicking down in Vera Cruz or somewhere.'

After a long searching moment, encouraged by Connery's levity, Vinnie smiled thinly. 'Monterrey – I have bought her a nice little *hacienda* there on a rise with a view . . . but I am truly sorry to hear about your boat, Captain. To show my good will, I will further reduce your rental. That is satisfactory. . . ?'

It was, but Connery couldn't help being suspicious. Vinnie always had to have his profit – but where could it be in this offer? Compassion or guilty conscience? Connery wondered. The hell with it: he was prepared to accept that burning the boat was Brock's own stupid idea.

'I want to clear town as soon as I can, Vinnie. Go hurry up your men, eh?'

Vinnie rose stiffly, reaching for the walking stick. 'Of course, Captain.'

Latigo, the man who was going to show Connery and his men how to handle the teams of oxen, was a small skinny man who wore two pistols and crossed bullet belts on his chest. He had an evil smile and a cast in one eye. With a battered full-size sombrero he looked more like a bandit chief than an ox-team driver. He was a man of about fifty, spoke politely, but those eyes were disconcerting and were never touched by his on-off smile.

He led the two wagons out of town, watched by Marshal Tigge who lounged in the doorway of his office, thumbs hooked in his gunbelt. Connery had reported the fire, figuring the sawbones would tell the lawman about Brock's wound. Anyway, he reckoned it wouldn't hurt to get in first, rather than have Tigge come riding out and stopping him along the trail. It was lucky he had made such a decision because Tigge had actually been on his way to Vinnie's warehouse when Connery had approached him.

'I've been waiting for someone to put a bullet in Brock. You might've finished it, save us both trouble in the long run.'

'And you'd've thrown me in jail.'

'Might still do it.' Then the marshal surprised Connery by smiling thinly. 'Only joshing – I figure you've had enough bad luck. You've never been in trouble while you were running the riverboat, so I'll make that count for something. When you rolling them wagons?'

All Tigge seemed interested in was getting the riverboat man out of town. He was an average-looking man, around forty, medium tall and build, soft spoken, and with a penetrating gaze. 'If I find out for sure Brock fired your boat, he'll be waiting in jail when you get back from Mexico.'

Connery nodded. 'Obliged, Marshal.'

The lawman added, 'I don't like vigilantes in my town, so don't plan on coming back to finish off Brock. You had your chance. Anything that happens to him now will be because of the law – and the way I see it.'

*

Some Mexicans from Nuevo Laredo just across the Rio had approached Connery about taking some of their goods, goods that they normally would have shipped on the *Rio Belle* on his scheduled stop. He took what he could but the wagons were pretty well loaded now and he had to refuse some work.

It hurt, because he needed every cent.

He hired mounts for himself, Ruben and McAllen, and the lumbering wagons cleared Laredo just before high noon, the mounts tied to the tailgates. Latigo and Connery were at the head of one team. A youth Latigo said was his son, Diego, led the other. McAllen and Ruben walking alongside. McAllen spat, swilled his mouth out with water from a canteen and growled, 'What's Connery's hurry? We coulda laid-over one more night.'

Ruben arched his eyebrows. 'It would've killed you, but I ain't noticed him hurryin' in particular.'

'Hell, he's runnin' round like a chicken with its head cut off. Can't get clear of Laredo fast enough.'

'He's had a helluva lot to do. That damn banker kept him on the hop and the marshal dogged him for a while . . . I don't blame him for wantin' to get on the trail in case Tigge changes his mind. Which he will do if Brock dies.'

'Ah, he'll live, tough *hombre* like him. Seems to me Connery's been in a hurry all along, even before the *Belle* wrecked. Kept sayin' he wanted to be in Brownsville by the seventeenth.'

Ruben snapped his head up. 'I never heard that.'

'You weren't workin' alongside him as much as me – you and Ace were busy takin' soundin's and splicin' ropes.'

Ruben shrugged: that was true enough. 'Well, he always likes to deliver on time and I guess he wants his money quick as he can.'

'Well, he's gonna be late, you ask me. We gotta get past Falcon Lake yet and that's over thirty mile long. Sailin' across was OK in a straight line, but now we're gonna have to follow the inland trail around it and these damn oxen won't be hurried.'

'They're strong as elephants, though.' Ruben squinted at McAllen. 'Why you worryin' about it, anyway?'

McAllen gave him a hard look. 'I want my money, too.'

'You know you'll get it – Clay Connery's no welsher.'

McAllen didn't answer but he knew that was true.

Because of a deep inlet at the lake, they lost time having to follow its edges and then drive the teams across the narrowest and shallowest part.

They couldn't have done it without Latigo and Diego, Connery knew that. The men were experts and they worked effortlessly – or so it seemed – apparently knowing the language used by oxen, for they could get the beasts to do whatever they wanted. It was even more remarkable because the youth was mute. But he could hear well enough and grinned in his usual friendly manner. Although he could not speak, he handled the teams as well, if not better, than his father, anticipating what the oxen had in mind, using his long-handled whip and a sapling he prodded the leaders with, making them go where he wanted.

They pushed the wagons hard and made camp the second night on the southern shores of the lake near another small inlet. Diego was a good cook and he and Latigo produced a fine Mexican meal, but the chilli in it had the Americans gasping. Latigo and Diego grinned at the *gringos'* discomfort.

Connery had had two cups of coffee and rose to walk around the camp-fire to the canteens of water. Breathing through his mouth to allow the cooler night air to soothe his burning throat, he stooped, picked up a canteen and worked off the screw cap. The cord which held it to the neck was broken and he didn't notice until he released his hold on the cap and it fell to the ground.

He took a quick mouthful and stooped quickly to pick up the cap. The felt-covered metal canteen jerked from his left hand, water exploding from it, and a moment later he heard the crack of the rifle out there in the darkness

He dropped flat as the rifle blasted three more times in quick succession and grass and twigs and gravel sprayed into his face as the bullets searched for him.

Then, as the men scattered, running for their own rifles, the gunman shifted aim and brought down one of the oxen just as Connery spotted the muzzle flashes. He triggered fast, just wanting to disconcert the bushwhacker. By then the others had their guns and they started blasting. The night was full of gunfire and shouting and the bawling of the oxen. And, finally, the hammering tattoo of a horse racing away into the night.

The Mexicans ran to the downed ox and Ruben started for his mount but Connery stopped him. 'Let him go. It's only one man – and there's no prizes for guessing who.'

McAllen frowned. 'Brock? Thought you hit him bad?'

Connery shrugged. 'Looked bad. Lot of blood and he was moaning plenty, but the bullet might've only skidded off a rib. Been two days since we quit Laredo. I reckon someone who hates as hard as Brock might've made an effort to come after us.'

The others looked doubtful, but had to admit it was a distinct possibilty.

The only thing was, he had missed Connery.

So he would be back.

CHAPTER 5

THE CAMARGO TRACE

They mounted night guards after the attack but nothing happened over the next couple of days. After they passed the south-eastern end of the lake they swung on to the old Camargo Trace which moved away from the river and led them towards Rio Grande City. It was a grand name for a small town with a strong mixture of Hispanic and Anglo in the population.

It was also a small army post, three troops of cavalry stationed at the fort on the south edge of town where they could also watch the river crossing to the twin town of Cuidad Camargo in Mexico. Connery hadn't had anything to do with the army post when sailing the *Rio Belle*, except one time he had been stopped and the boat had been searched briefly for some fugitive.

So he was some surprised when the wagons crunched and rocked and swayed down the well-worn trail just outside of Rio Grande City and a troop of soldiers came riding in, signalling him to stop. Latigo and Diego soon brought the teams to a halt and Connery, mounted at that time, rode out ahead to meet the soldiers.

There was a lieutenant in charge and he was a small-eyed arrogant type with waxed ends to his moustache and a uniform the creases of which could have cut a man's finger deep enough to require stitches. He was in his forties and perhaps had no reason to think he would advance any further than his present rank, stationed out here on this relatively law-abiding part of the river.

'You're who?' was his greeting as Connery reined in.

The freighter told him his name briefly and said no more, realizing this man was going to do everything by the book and make things difficult for him.

'Destination? Freight manifests?' The lieutenant snapped his fingers and, as Connery dug into his pocket, he saw that the soldiers were sitting their mounts ramrod stiff. The sergeant spoke quietly but firmly to the man carrying the guidon. This man's face reddened and he hurriedly straightened the staff so that it was pefectly perpendicular.

The lieutenant didn't take off his polished leather gauntlets and fumbled the papers, one falling and blowing away across the sparse grass. The man merely looked at Connery who started to call to Ruben, but Diego was already diving for the paper, retrieved it and handed it up to Connery with his usual friendly smile.

'Give me that!' the lieutenant snapped, and Connery handed it over without speaking, the officer glaring at Diego. He shuffled the papers, looked up at Connery. 'Nowhere does it say that you have Mexicans employed.'

'Didn't know it had to.'

'Ignorance is no excuse. Your Mexicans should be listed here together with their remuneration. Bring your wagons into the post. No doubt the captain will want to see you.'

'Wasn't aiming to go through the town, Lieutenant. We're in kind of a hurry to get to Brownsville.'

'And Matamoros, no doubt.'

Connery nodded.'We have goods for there, yes.'

'You like dealing with Mexicans?'

'I take them as I find them – some good, some not so good, some downright bad. Just like white folk.'

The small eyes grew even smaller. 'Ah, we have us a bleeding-heart liberal here, I see. Sergeant! Direct these wagons to the post and take four men for escort.'

He wheeled his mount and rode off. The sergeant, a craggy-faced man of about fifty who looked as if he had seen everything there was to see on the border frontier, snapped his orders and chose the four men for escort. The rest hurriedly rode after the lieutanant, the guidon carrier moving on ahead, trying to catch up with the officer.

The wagons turned away from the Trace and

started for Rio Grande City. Connery rode slowly, waiting to see if the sergeant was any friendlier than the officer. He was, the man dropping back alongside Connery's mount.

'Sergeant Ames.'

'Clay Connery.'

'Yeah – recognize you. You had the *Rio Belle*, didn't you?'

Connery nodded, told him what had happened.

'Too bad. You picked a bad time to travel this side of the river on land, though.'

'How come?'

'Haven't you heard about the big robbery? – No, guess you wouldn't've if you were comin' down-river when your boat sank. Happened about two weeks ago. Army train to Corpus Christi out of San Antone – derailed, hit by Indians and a group of masked men, white or Mex, no one's too sure. Killed everyone and got away with eight Gatling guns and some boxes of Trapdoor Springfields, with ammo for both. They reckon Mex bandits are behind it, but they don't really know.'

Connery whistled. 'This why your lieutenant's acting so hard?'

'He's always been hard-nosed, but the shavetail loot in charge of that train was his kid brother.'

'Uh-huh. So he's enforcing this thing about Mexicans having a work ticket and – what else can I expect?'

'Well, Captain Havelock's mostly OK – when he's not takin' his *medicine*, if you know what I mean – but there's pressure on him. Word is that they smuggled the Gatlings across the Rio between here and the mission outside of Reynosa – which puts it right in our patrol area.'

Connery swore. 'More delays then, I guess. I hope his damn search won't mean off-loading. Those Conestogas are carrying maximum load.'

'I'd say loosen up your muscles, Connery.'

'Well, hell, a blind man can see we don't have anything the size of a Gatling gun hidden.'

'Not just the guns he's lookin' for – there's ammo and spare parts. Afraid you're in for quite a delay.'

'Goddamnit! I'm running behind schedule already!'

Which didn't cut any ice with Captain Havelock. On the advice of the lieutenant, whose name was de Witt, he ordered a 'thorough and complete search of the wagons'. Connery protested but his complaints fell on deaf ears. The captain, a man near retirement, looked haggard and impatient for the riverboat man to clear his office. He kept looking towards a deep desk drawer, hands trembling a little.

The room smelled strongly of brandy and Connery figured there would be no arguing with this man – not until he had a couple of hefty slugs of liquor under his belt, anyway. Then his moods could go either way.

So, resignedly, they waited for the remainder of the day while a bunch of soldiers off-loaded the freight and opened everything that could be opened. But when they wanted to knock the upper hoops off the casks of tallow and tar and wine, Connery exploded and Captain Havelock, his nerves by then soothed by brandy, merely waved a hand and slurred,

'Very well, very well – You've co – co-operrrrated well until now. . . .'

'Captain, I must protest!' said Lieutenant de Witt, who had been overseeing the whole thing. 'Gun parts could be hidden in those casks! Even a Gatling's barrels or stand. . . .'

'Oh, you're supposed to be off-duty, Lieutenant,' the captain said irritably. 'Go to your quarters and wax your muss-tache or something.'

As de Witt coloured almost to the stage of apoplexy, Havelock giggled, waved a hand languidly and went back into his office, talking to himself.

De Witt fumed and his gauntleted hands clenched and unclenched down at his sides as Connery and his men began to reload the wagons.

'Could use a couple of strong backs with these casks, Lieutenant,' Connery said, and de Witt looked at him coldly.

'I am relieved of duty – make your own arrange-ments with Sergeant Ames.' De Witt stormed away towards the officers' quarters and Connery approached the sergeant who was grinning crookedly.

'Good postin' this,' he said wryly. 'If we ain't pullin' the captain outa the hoss trough and pourin' him into bed, we're paintin' stones, or sortin' coal into sizes, or polishin' our boots till de Witt can see hisself in 'em.'

'Must make life interesting,' Connery opined. 'How about those men to help load? – I can spare 'em a couple of dollars. I see you've got a sutler's on post. . . .'

Aimes licked his lips.'There's better and cheaper places in town. But you got yourself a deal, Connery, and I'll even show you where you can sleep the night.'

There was no choice but to accept Ames's offer as it was full dark by the time the wagons were reloaded.

But Connery had them on the trail again so early that they were barely within earshot of the post when reveille was finally sounded to start the army's day.

Connery cursed the delay – but that wasn't the only delay he would meet along the Camargo Trace.

It was hot and dusty work and reminded Connery of his trail-herding days – even the bawling of the oxen wasn't out of place, and the creak and grind of the Conestogas could have been the chuckwagon and the gear wagon.

But he was far south of the cattle trails and the Rio was in sight to their right. A paddle-steamer crawled by, stern-wheel churning, whistles blasting white ribbons of steam, instantly shredded by the wind, on the smokestacks.

'That ain't Keller, is it?' asked McAllen, standing on the seat of the wagon he was riding with Ruben, shading his eyes.

'Too early for him to have made turn-around if he was goin' to Del Rio,' Rubin allowed. 'But he ought-n't to be far behind.'

'I hope Connery's gonna square-up to him over the *Belle*.'

'We'll see, but the cap ain't ever backed down as far as I know.'

'He's got somethin' else on his mind, these days,' McAllen said slowly. 'I tell you, makin' that deadline he's set for Brownsville's got somethin' to do with it. . . .'

Ruben had lost interest and sucked on an empty corncob pipe, feeling his pockets for a little tobacco he might have missed on previous searches.

They were within five or six miles of the old mission north-east of Reynosa, approaching sundown on the second day after leaving Rio Grande City. The air was humid and the skies leaden, big-bellied clouds beginning to turn a pink-gold as the sun sank and the rays fanned out from behind the low ranges. Latigo had told Connery there was a *laguna* at a place called Sereno, reached by way of a short narrow cutting where they could bed down for the night.

McAllen griped as usual.

'Why don't we keep goin' far as the mission? I mean, we can get a decent bed and the grub them monks eat maybe ain't fancy but there's always plenty of it.'

'We're swinging south of the mission, Mac,' Connery told him. 'Heading down to Reynosa.'

McAllen muttered to himself about 'crazy damn trail to take' but by now the wagons were heading through the cutting, the gleam of flatwater showing beyond the end, and the call of homing birds just reaching them.

Until the first volley of gunfire drowned them out.

Dust spurted from the hides of at least four oxen and the big, heavy beasts snorted and bellowed before their legs collapsed under them and their noses ploughed into the dusty trail.

McAllen and Ruben, still riding the second wagon, rolled back under the arched canvas hood, groping for their guns, as another volley shredded that same canvas, and lead whined and spanged amongst the freight.

Diego at the head of the line of oxen where two had collapsed, started to run but rifle fire cut him down in mid-stride. Latigo saw it and cried out in anguish, running towards his son. Dust spurted about his sandalled feet and he fell sprawling.

Connery was the only one mounted and he spun his horse, snatching his rifle from its scabbard. Lead punched dust from the stiff brim of his hat and he stretched along the mount's neck as it laid back its ears and responded to the raking of his spurs. He rammed it in amongst some rocks and quit leather fast, slapping the animal's rump with his hat, sending it deeper into cover while he threw himself full length. He quickly drew up his long legs as bullets spattered around them, one flicking a loose trouser cuff.

The attackers, of course, were up on the rim of the cutting, but seemed to be only on one side, that nearest the river, a bend of which was in sight from here. He ducked as rock dust sprayed into his face, and then laid his sights on the rim. A man's arms and shoulders showed against the glowing skyline as he eased forward so as to get a better shot at Connery sprawled amongst the rocks. Connery triggered, levered, triggered again.

The first bullet punched the man almost upright and the second slammed into his body. He shuddered, dropped his rifle over the edge – then doubled up and followed it down without a sound, until he struck rocks below and Connery knew he would never move again.

But by that time the man's pards were raking Connery's shelter and he huddled close to the sandstone. Ruben and McAllen opened up, Ruben using the twelve-gauge Greener, emptying first one barrel, then the other. Explosions of rock chips and dirt were flung from the edge in two places. A man screamed and McAllen glimpsed him as he clawed at his bloody face with both hands. McAllen shot the man through the head. He swung his sights to the next target and clipped a shoulder, spinning the attacker violently.

Someone screamed orders in Spanish, high-pitched, urgent, perhaps even frightened. Guns raked the Conestoga beneath which Ruben and McAllen lay. Latigo, wounded it seemed, had managed to drag Diego beneath the first wagon and was smoothing the boy's hair. Ruben couldn't see if Diego was alive or not.

A savage volley raked the wagons and Connery's shelter and when they heard levers and bolt-actions working on empty magazines, they fired a heavy volley in return, shooting until their Winchesters were empty.

While they reloaded, the attackers started firing again and there seemed to be more now – maybe that Spaniard had called for reinforcements.

Then they heard a bugle's notes, loud and sweet and clarion-clear, as the gunsmoke drifted in dirty clouds across the late afternoon.

A troop of cavalry came thundering in, the clatter of hoofs drowned in the thunder of their heavy Trapdoor Springfield rifles. A pistol sounded, too, and the rapid crack of a repeating rifle.

Connery and the others didn't try to identify their rescuers, poured fire at the cutting's rim and another body came hurtling down to thud into the ground near the bawling ox team of the closest Conestoga.

The cavalry swept past, dividing, half the men heading for the far end of the cutting, the rest sweeping around the other end, aiming to cut off the retreat of the bandits.

Connery ran towards the closest end, hearing the sounds of savage gunfire from beyond. He slipped twice and when he clambered over the rocks and was far enough around to see a bunch of men retreating fast towards the distant river, pursued by cavalry, he stopped, panting, wiping gritty powder grains from his face.

The army had it well in hand.

He sat down on a flat rock, getting his breath as Ruben and McAllen came panting up. He was about to speak when a soldier rode over, hauling rein on his lathered mount. It was Sergeant Ames.

'Welcome, Sarge!' Connery gasped, grinning.

Ames dismounted and moved his gaze over the three of them. 'No one hurt?' He sounded surprised.

'Maybe the young Mexican,' Ruben said and

Connery snapped up his head. 'Latigo's hit, too, but not bad, I think.'

Connery stood but Ames placed a hand on his arm. 'We got word there was some *bandidos* crossin' the Rio and gonna hit your wagons at the laguna or the mission. Guess they got impatient and made their try while you were still in the cuttin'.'

Connery nodded. 'Who sent you after us?'

'De Witt – he might be a pain in the ass and a pompous son of a bitch, but he's a good soldier. Havelock was passed out in a drunken stupory. I reckon he's about finished . . . glad we got here in time.'

'So're we – but why did they pick my wagons? You get much trouble with bandits crossin' the Rio to hit wagon trains along here?'

Ames shook his head. 'Not often but it does happen. Let's take a look at these fellers you shot.'

The first two were Mexicans and Ames said one was a well-known bandit on both sides of the river. But when they turned over the white man Connery had shot off the rim, the riverboat man swore. Ames looked at him sharply.

'Know him?'

'Yeah. Turk Harmon. Keller's first mate on the *Blade*.'

CHAPTER 6

BORDER TOWN

Diego, shot twice through the back, one bullet clipping a lung, was taken into Reynosa by Ames's men. Latigo had been shot in one arm and went with him, apologizing before going in courteous fashion for leaving Connery in the lurch.

'Go with the boy, Latigo. Will you need money?'

'No, *señor*.' He hesitated, and then turned back. '*Capitan* – You are the best *gringo* I have work for. I work for Señor Vincenz because I owe him a debt. . . .' He paused again but Connery could see that more was coming. 'I therefore do what he asks. You will recall before we left Laredo I insisted that you draw me a rough map of the trail you wished to take?'

Connery remembered: it had annoyed him at the time but the request had seemed reasonable enough, seeing as Latigo would be working the ox teams.

'I – it was on the *jefe*'s orders that I ask this. And he wish to see it . . . so I show him before we leave Laredo.'

Connery didn't like that and felt himself tensing

up. 'Go on, Latigo.'

'I have done many things for the *jefe* because I owe him much and I must do what I can to reduce my debt. He was most interested in the trail near the mission and said I should make sure you watered the teams at the *laguna*. . . .'

'And to get there, we had to go through that cutting,' said Connery thoughtfully. 'You think he could've arranged that ambush?'

Latigo shrugged. 'This I do not know, Captain. But Señor Vincenz has his fingers in many things. And whoever arranged it, did not intend for anyone to come out alive, I think.'

'You're right there – Sergeant Ames arrived just in time. His men said the bandits got away across the Rio in waiting boats. They left one large punt-type behind – the kind you'd use to ferry goods across the river. And there were tools in it – hammers, chisels, pry-bars.'

Latigo nodded. 'I am ashamed, *señor* – I may even have caused the death of my own son!'

Connery touched the man on the arm, feeling the stringy muscle beneath the ragged shirt. 'He'll be all right, Latigo. Now you get going with him and the soldiers. I don't hold anything against you – *gracias* for telling me.'

They couldn't move the wagons with what was left of the oxen. Four had been killed outright and two more had to be shot to end their suffering. If they harnessed all the animals left to one Conestoga they could probably get it along the trail, but it would be mighty hard and slow work and meant leaving the other wagon behind. So Connery left Ruben and McAllen to guard

70

the wagons, with three soldiers provided by Ames, and told them he was riding into Brownsville.

'Why the hell you goin' all the way to Brownsville?' asked McAllen. 'Reynosa's closer, or even Rio Bravo.'

'More likely to pick up oxen in Brownsville, with their big Mex population, and I can ride fast. Besides, we're not going to make it in by the seventeenth with the wagons but I reckon I can get there in time on a horse. If bandits come back, let 'em have the wagons and hightail it to the mission. You'll be safe there.'

Both McAllen and Ruben reacted to this.

'Just leave all them goods to a bunch of greasers? You're loco, Skipper!'

'You'll be broke, Cap, and you'll owe Vinnie for the wagons and teams as well,' Ruben pointed out.

'Just let 'em take what they want – not worth getting yourselves shot over.' Connery mounted and nodded briefly. 'Be back as quick as I can.'

McAllen lifted his hat and scratched his head as he watched Connery spur the mount away. 'Now what in singein' hell is he *up* to?'

'He's definitely got somethin' special on in Brownsville on the seventeenth, Mac. Somethin' he ain't told us about – an' ain't likely to by the looks of things.'

Mac spat, scowling. 'Why would he? He's still the son-of-a-bitchin' captain!'

Ruben looked at McAllen soberly. 'He's a damn good cap'n, Mac, he's always treated us fair. Don't grudge him somethin' that likely ain't none of our business anyway.'

McAllen grunted. 'Coulda told us,' he muttered.

'*Coulda* done, Rube!'

Mac sounded quite hurt and Ruben was surprised to realize that for all of McAllen's endless bitching and criticism, he was still loyal to Connery and liked the big man a lot more than he was letting on.

Covered in a thick layer of trail grit, smelling of man-sweat and horses, stiff from long hours of hard riding, Connery made straight for the cattle-holding pens down by the river docks when he rode into Brownsville in the middle of a hot and sultry afternoon.

The pens were crowded with bawling cattle and cursing cowboys as they worked them into loading chutes and hazed them on to the wide, low decks of a paddle-steamer. It was one of King's, of course, *Spanish Dancer*, and it was a hive of activity. Connery climbed through the bars of the pens, pushed and shoved his way through milling, bawling cows, looking at the various brands. They had come in from all over Texas for auction here in Brownsville. Some would go up-river, others would be driven across to Matamoros and overland south to the beef-hungry towns along the *Laguna Madre* – it was a mighty lucrative business, selling cattle here.

There were many different brands. Lazy Q, Standing T, Rocking W, Broken Heart – he wondered what stories that one could tell! – Wagon Wheel, Cross Knives, Box Double L and, finally, the one he wanted, Sawtooth.

He grinned to himself and fought his way over to the fence again, ducking through the rails, stopping a sweating wrangler.

'Yuma Shannon. Seen him about anywhere?'

The man peered at Connery's clothes closely. 'Where I seen him they wouldn't let you past the front door.'

'I scrub up pretty good – is he still in town?'

The cowboy caught the urgency in Connery's voice and nodded slowly. 'Far as I know – up to the Bijou on River Street.'

Connery was already moving away, hurrying, taking off his hat and slapping dust from his clothes. He paused at a horse trough and sluiced his face and hair, washing the back of his neck, drying off on a well-used neckerchief. Some of the folk on the crowded street stopped to watch but none seemed all that interested. Brownsville was a bustling town and folk hurried about their own business, no time for anyone else's.

The wrangler was right, the front desk clerk at Bijou did not want to let Connery into the foyer let alone up the stairs to Yuma Shannon's room. The clerk banged a counter-top bell and a big man whose muscles and hard body bulged a good quality frock-coat and striped trousers came across, brittle eyes summing-up Connery at a glance. The clerk didn't have to give him any instructions.

The bouncer knew his target from long experience and he reached quickly for Connery's arm, fingers already clawed, ready to bite into flesh and sinew. Except that the big clawed hand never touched Connery. The bouncer grunted and gasped in shocked pain and jumped back as Connery's sixgun slid out of leather and the barrel slapped the hand aside, breaking the skin and bruising a few bones. There was a sudden stillness and silence in the hotel foyer.

The bouncer's reputation was on the line and he knew it, shook the bleeding, injured hand, snarled, and rushed in. Connery stepped to one side, gun-whipped the man across the side of the head, driving him to his knees. He grabbed the man's collar and held him from falling on his face as he looked at the white-faced clerk.

'No need for any of this – just send up for Yuma Shannon. Tell him Clay Connery wants to see him.'

'Hell, I mighta known it was you causin' a disturbance in the foyer of the best hotel in town.'

A silver-haired man in a pale-grey outfit, with a dark-skinned woman in a green and white dress on his left arm, was coming down the stairs, grinning around a fat cigar.

Connery let the barely conscious bouncer fall, stepped over him and holstered his gun before he reached the bottom of the stairs. He held out his right hand and the big man with the silver-grey hair shook enthusiastically. He turned to the woman, said something in a low voice and patted her hand. She looked briefly annoyed, shot Connery a curious glance, then turned and, lifting her skirts, showing a fine pair of well-turned ankles, hurried back up the stairs. The clerk started around the desk but Shannon waved the man back.

'Clay, you stink worse'n that hoss we shared when them Piutes was after us at Painted Rock that time!'

'Rode a long way in a short time, Yuma, just to see you.'

'Well, we better go renew acquaintances over a few

74

drinks.' He stooped and pushed a gold coin into the bouncer's jacket pocket, then led the way through an ornate archway into a smoke-filled but quiet room with padded chairs set around a series of small tables. They took a vacant corner table and Shannon ordered a bottle of whiskey from the Mexican waiter – *'From my stock'* – and offered Connery a cigar.

'Bit too rich for me, Yuma. I see your Sawtooth brand's still holding its own. Good fat cows down at the pens.'

'That where you picked up that stink? Boy, I think we better get you to a bath-house after one or two of these.'

He indicated the glasses of whiskey and Connery tossed his down, poured another. 'Or three or four.'

'You need something, Clay?' Yuma asked quietly.

Connery looked at him over the rim of his glass and nodded slightly, setting down the drink untouched. 'Swore I'd never take you up on your offer, Yuma, but – I'm between a rock and a hard place right now and don't seem to be going anywhere but down.'

Shannon sipped his drink, sat back in his chair and spread his hands expansively. 'Whatever it is, I'm just mighty glad of the chance to pay back something of what I owe you, Clay.'

Connery held up a hand. 'Wait a spell now, till you find out what it is.'

The silver head shook slowly. 'Don't care what it is – if it'll help you, it's yours. And I mean *anything*.'

Connery's lips compressed. 'Damnit, that's just why I've never come near you since—'

'Since you saved my neck and my family as well when those rioters burned down our house just because we happened to live on the same street as the lousy land agent who cheated them out of their money. . . .'

Connery gave him a level stare. 'I heard your wife left you.'

'Few years ago – no hard feelings. She just couldn't take my style of living and I sure as hell couldn't handle hers. So – parting of the ways. Young Glenda's a governess at a *hacienda* in Mexico and Sidney, believe it or not, took to cattle buying like me, got his own family now. So, c'mon Clay, tell me what it is you need.'

Connery still hesitated. *If luck hadn't been with him that night he won the boat he might have ended up on Shannon's doorstep long before this, hat in hand, taking up the open invitation Yuma had given him after he had dragged the man's family out of the burning house – and almost died of pneumonia as a result of inhaling the thick smoke.*

But they had been friends for a long time before that, had ridden the cattle trails together, occasionally bending the law, including the time the Piutes almost caught them at Painted Rock, prospecting on their land. Then Connery had decided to try ranching and bought that cheap place in Arizona. He was slowly going broke when the trail-driving job with Anniston had come along and eventually led him to the winning of the *Rio Belle*.

Yuma had been an ordinary cowpoke, too, but instead of buying land with his share of the Indian gold had taken a gamble and bought a small herd off a man who had been badly wounded along the trail by rustlers. He had driven the cows to a town that had been cut off by floods for weeks – and the people would pay anything for beef. It was there that Yuma had discovered he had a knack for cattle trading and he had become one of the biggest and most success-ful cattle agents in the South-west.

He and Connery had met a couple of times over the years and one of those times Shannon had taken him to the large house he had built on a rise over-looking the Colorado River with a view right up a green-and-gold valley. A rich, beautiful and peaceful place. Until they had gone on the town, celebrating, and returned to find a rioting mob, after burning down the mansion belonging to the crooked land developer, had set fire to Shannon's house. Shannon had been knocked unconscious by some of the rioters – and Connery had become a hero by rushing into the flames and dragging the Shannon family to safety.

Then he had gone back for Shannon and arrived in time to stop a couple of drunks robbing him – and trying to kick him to death at the same time. He shot them both and got Yuma Shannon out of there.

Now it was time to collect his reward.

He hated himself for even thinking like that! But it was true – and he was just desperate enough to stake his claim after all those years.

So he told Shannon about the *Rio Belle* and its fate – and how he was now deep in debt to Vinnie Vincenz.

'That two-timer! Clay, you must've been mighty desperate! You damn fool, why didn't you get in touch right away?'

'I had thought about it – I heard there was a big cattle auction here on the seventeenth and that you had some of your own herds in it. Figured I might look you up. But Keller ran me aground and fixed that notion.' He shrugged. 'Then after the wagon ambush I decided to ride ahead and see if you were still here.'

Shannon shook his head. 'Man, I'd've been more'n happy to help you out – bought you a new boat if that's what you wanted. 'But – to get mixed up with Vinnie! Can't believe you'd do that.'

'Well, I'd done a little – *business* with him before, up and down the river.'

'Christ, Clay, what's wrong with you? Why'd you have to take risks like that when you knew all you had to do was ask me and I'd've—'

'That's why I didn't ask, Yuma. It was too easy and you didn't really owe me anything.'

'You call saving me and my family *nothing*? Jesus!'

'You know what I mean – I've always made my own way. Never beholden to any man. But somehow I took to riverboat trading and I always had the ranch in the back of my mind, figuring to go back to it after I'd made enough money on the river. I'm still a cattleman at heart.'

Shannon insisted they go to a bath-house and they shared a room, with a frothy hip bath each, declining the services of some eager, blowsy womenfolk who eventually sulked away muttering uncomplimentary things about cheapskates. Shannon ordered more booze and Mexican kids brought more pails of hot water on request. Connery's aching bones appreciated the heat soaking away the weariness and stiffness.

He stayed much longer in the bath than Shannon, who sat with a towel wrapped round his waist, smoking another fat cigar, while he waited for Connery to get through.

'Vinnie must've arranged that ambush,' he said flatly, watching Connery's face closely as the man looked at him through soap bubbles. 'You're carrying contraband whether you know it or not. That was Vinnie's way of getting back at you for throwing him down the stairs and avoiding having to pay you anything for carrying whatever it is down to Mexico. He tipped the bandits so they could take it off you and likely kill you into the bargain. Only way it can be, Clay.'

Connery was feeling the effects of the whiskey but his head was clear enough to follow Shannon's reasoning.

'I thought much the same thing – but De Witt's men practically tore those Conestoga's apart, Yuma, and they found nothing. If Vinnie somehow planted contraband on me, I'm damned if I know where it is—'

'You need to get the wagons in here.'

Connery grinned crookedly. 'Sure – if you'll help me hire some oxen and find me a couple more men to help.'

'Done. – but what then? You want, I can have a coach builder I know reduce those Conestogas to planks and bolts.'

'No. I've got goods to deliver to Matamoros and further south, Yuma – I'm running late, but I promised to get 'em there and I will.'

'You're going to risk crossing the border? Hell, if the Mexes find contraband hidden in the wagons you won't see daylight for twenty years!'

'Well, if the army couldn't find anything. . . .'

'Not worth the risk, feller! Hell, I'll grubstake you for whatever you want, that's for sure, but it's plumb loco to even think of taking those wagons over the border.'

Connery didn't feel like arguing about it any more, changed the subject and got out of the bath. Shannon had sent out one of the Mexicans for new shirt and trousers for Connery, had had his comfortable but worn riding boots cleaned and several hats brought in so Connery could select one that suited.

They went to a restaurant on Imperial Street where they ate a pretty good meal – and put away a few more drinks. Shannon bought some regular-sized cigars and Connery accepted one of these. It was as he was bending his head towards the light that Shannon held for him, that he glanced towards the street entrance and saw a man and a woman coming in.

She was the same dark-skinned woman who had been with Shannon earlier, on the stairs at the Bijou.

He was about to draw the cattle-buyer's attention to this when he looked again at the man, who was fully in the light now.

It was Keller, of the riverboat *Blade*.

CHAPTER 7

THE WRECKERS

'Who is that woman?' Connery asked, but watching Keller as he looked around for a table.

'Consuela – she's a kind of Bijou *companion* to guests and visiting cattlemen or riverboat men—' Yuma stopped suddenly, looking sharply at Connery. 'You know who he is, don't you?'

'Uh-huh.' Connery stood slowly, putting down his unlit cigar. 'And I'm about to make his reacquaintance.'

Shannon placed a restraining hand on his arm. 'Don't do it, Clay, not in here. Sheriff Griffin runs a tight town.'

'That son of a bitch deliberately ran me aground and destroyed my boat, Yuma. Can't let this go.'

Shannon dropped his hand and nodded. 'Knowing you, I guess not, but—'

It was too late anyway. Connery was striding across the restaurant and, at the same time as a waiter was holding a chair for Consuela, Keller looked around casually – and saw Connery.

He stiffened and the woman looked up quickly as did the waiter. The man paled and said something to Keller but the riverboat captain knew this coming fight was inevitable and he swung up the chair the waiter was pulling out for him, shoved the man aside and charged across the room. Other diners gave cries of alarm and one woman swooned away. Men jumped to to their feet. Keller's waiter started to run for the kitchen, shouting in rapid Spanish.

Connery dodged the first blow with the chair. The legs shattered against the edge of a table and the two women screamed and the men, both in dinner suits jumped up, shouting protests. Keller stabbed at them with the remains of the chair and one fell against the other, then tumbled over his own chair, pulling the cloth and dinner plates and cups off the table.

The room was in chaos even before the antagonists met. Connery ducked under the swinging chair and rammed the top of his head into Keller's square face. The riverboat captain dropped the remains of the chair and blood squirted from his mashed nose. Connery, feeling the whiskey he had consumed, was a little slow, but he landed a good, solid blow on the side of Keller's jaw. It was hard enough to turn the man's head violently and he rolled across the table, taking it with him to the floor.

He snatched the loose tablecloth as more utensils and cutlery clattered to the floor, whipped it around Connery's lower legs and pulled hard. Connery went down with a thud, arms flailing, trying to kick his legs free. Keller launched himself on top of the freighter and sledged two hard blows into Connery's face.

The man shook his head, ears ringing, the coppery taste of blood in his mouth. He rolled away from Keller as the man tried to ram the point of an elbow into his throat. He took the bony point on his shoulder, kicked out and landed a boot on Keller's chest. He twisted away as Keller fell. Connery lay on his back, kicked at Keller's head, missed, drove both boots together into the man's side as he rolled to the left.

Keller skidded into the overturned table and by the time he had hauled himself to his knees, Connery was up and driving a knee into his face. Keller hurtled backwards, rolled off the angled table and then scrabbled quickly out of range on hands and knees. He leapt up as if driven by a spring, got his hands up in time to ward off a barrage of blows from Connery, retreating and dodging wildly. Connery kept up the pressure, storming forward, refusing to stop even though his fists were battering only Keller's forearms. And then Keller missed his rhythm and a blow tore through and snapped his head back on his shoulders.

He reeled and one arm dropped, groping for support. Another of Connery's blows tore through the opening, flattening an ear against Keller's head. The man shouted in raw pain, clapped both hands to that ear. Connery crouched, darted in, fists moving like pistons, cracking Keller's ribs, sinking into his mid-section, whistling in an uppercut that hurled the man into another table. He spilled to the floor, awkwardly tried to escape, but Connery was unstoppable, kicked the table aside, and two chairs, splintering one, strode in and hammered a battering barrage into the riverboat-captain's body, grunting with the force of each blow.

Keller stumbled and floundered, put down a hand to stop from falling completely – and found his fingers closing around the neck of a wine bottle. He bared his bloody teeth and hurled it at Connery's head. The man ducked and when he straightened he saw that Keller had found a second bottle. The riverboat captain smashed it against the edge of a table.

Red wine sprayed like a fan of blood and shattered glass slivers flashed in the lamplight. Connery's head was roaring with sound: his own blood pumping wildly, people shouting, women screaming, wood splintering – and now glass breaking. An instant later the jagged ends of the bottle were thrust at his face.

He hauled his head and upper body swiftly aside, smashed out with the heel of his right hand. It slapped against Keller's rigid wrist, turning the broken bottle aside. Connery followed through by driving the heel of his left hand against the back of Keller's head. The man staggered and Connery rushed him, forcing him back fast, driving him face first into the wall. There was an audible crack of cartilage, the sickening thump of a forehead hitting wood and the skin splitting from hairline to nose bridge.

Keller was dazed, on his way out, but Connery turned him with a brutal punch to one shoulder, the man's back slamming against the wall. His legs were folding and he began to slide down.

Connery set his boots wide apart, breathing heavily through his own bleeding nostrils as he set himself and hammered blow after blow into the man all the way to the floor. Then he drew back his right leg and slammed the boot into the unconscious man's ribs.

He was setting himself for yet another kick when Yuma grabbed him by both shoulders, held him and gave him a shake.

'Don't kill him, you damn fool!' Shannon gritted.

Connery looked at him without recognition for a moment, eyes red and flaring with a murderous madness that faded slowly as Shannon righted a chair and pushed him down into it.

'Not worth swinging for a bastard like Keller,' the cattle agent said, handing Connery a bottle of whiskey.

The freighter's chest was heaving and the bottle neck rattled against his blood-smeared teeth but he took a long pull, nodded, and held out the bottle to Yuma.

'Have another in a minute.' Shannon looked around at the shambles of the room. 'Hell, man, you've demolished half the restaurant!'

Connery saw it through one swollen eye and a more or less good one filling with fluid of some kind. There were broken chairs, overturned tables, crumpled cloths, scattered cutlery and broken plates and dishes and cups. Spilled and trampled food made the floor slippery and dangerous. Connery just about had enough breath left to whistle through aching teeth and saw the frantic, gesticulating owner, dragging in Sheriff Griffin, a hard-eyed deputy coming up behind.

Griffin took one look around, his gaze passing over the bloody, unconscious Keller, settling on the bloody and not-much-more-conscious Connery slumped in the chair with Yuma Shannon standing beside him.

The lawman walked across, a man in his late thirties, built like a tree trunk with practically no neck at all, and a face that had met more than a few fists over the years. He wore a single sixgun set for a cross draw and his right hand was flexing thick fingers as he came up. The deputy, long, lean and mean-looking, hurried across, cradling a long-barrelled Ithaca shotgun the yawning muzzles of which told Connery it was loaded with 12 gauge, likely in double-o buckshot.

Griffin nodded to Shannon. 'Friend of yours, Yuma?'

'Uh-huh – and he had a big score to settle with Keller. The man ran his keelboat aground off Laredo a week ago and he lost his livelihood.'

'We all have a run of bad luck,' Griffin said, eyes narrowing as he looked at Connery. 'Heard a little about it – you'd be Connery.'

'I am.'

'What gave you the idea you could come into my town and start tearin' it up?'

Connery made a helpless gesture. 'I just wanted to smash-up Keller, Sheriff – the other stuff just kinda got in the way.'

Griffin glanced around the shambles briefly. 'I'd say it did.' Then his hand flashed across his body and the Colt whispered out of leather and the hammer cocked back as the muzzle pointed rock-steady at Connery who looked up, frowning. 'On your feet – we've got a spare cell tonight and it's all yours.'

'Wait up, Griff!' Yuma said quickly. 'You can't jail Clay for this – I'll pay for any damage to the restaurant.'

Connery started to say something, likely a protest, but Griffin, without looking at him, raised a hand, palm outwards.

'Quiet! Yuma, I ain't arrestin' this ranny for any damage he's done to the restaurant, or for beatin'-up on Keller . . . arrogant sonuver likely deserved it.'

Shannon looked puzzled, spreading his hands. 'Then what are you arresting him for?'

Griffin's face was rock-hard as he shifted his gaze from the cattle agent to Connery.

'Murder,' he said flatly.

Sitting on the edge of the hard bunk in the cell, Connery leaned his elbows on his knees while the doctor placed some strips of adhesive plaster over a couple of cuts on his face. The medic had put two stitches in a deep gash above his left eye, set his nose painfully, but it looked straight again, even if it was a mite swollen and red.

Tight-lipped, Sheriff Griffin stood at the cell door with his hand on his sixgun. Yuma Shannon waited impatiently beside him and the deputy with the shotgun lounged in the doorway at the end of the passage that led to the front office.

'You about through, Doc?' asked Griffin gratingly, and the doctor nodded, began to put his things away.

87

He looked at Connery.

'Those ribs are going to be sore for a few days. I'd recommend rest.'

Griffin laughed harshly. 'He's gonna get plenty of that – until his trial, leastways.'

He opened the door to let the doctor out, holding his Colt now, but Connery didn't move off the bunk.

'I'd like to know who I'm s'posed to've murdered, Sheriff,' Connery said, his speech sounding a little thick because of puffy and split lips.

Yuma wondered just how Keller must be feeling – after all he was the loser and in worse shape than Connery. He stopped the doctor as he made his way down the passage.

'Send the bill to me, Doc.'

The sawbones nodded and continued on towards the front office where the unsmiling deputy stood to one side and allowed him to pass.

The sheriff leaned against the bars and rolled a cigarette, taking his time. 'How about a man named Brock?'

Connery's shoulders stiffened. 'How about him?'

'He's the man you murdered.'

Connery started to get up but it hurt too much and he slumped back, resting against the cold stone wall now. He shook his head slowly.

'I had a sort of gunfight with Brock in Laredo but I only winged him. Could've killed him and was going to but changed my mind – he didn't need killng so much as a lesson to show him he wasn't as tough as he figured. I knew he was just acting on orders from Vinnie Vincenz, burning my boat.'

'Now *that's* a man *I* wouldn't brag about even if I did know him – but never mind Vinnie. Brock's the man who died and there are witnesses who'll say you never gave him a chance, just drew your Colt and shot him.'

'What witnesses?'

'Three Mexicans who work in Vinnie's freight warehouse.'

'Hell, they'd say whatever Vinnie told 'em to! Be too afraid not to.'

'That's as mebbe, but the fact is they all agree on the same story and you shot Brock down cold – one of his wounds proved fatal.'

Connery stood up this time and, grimacing and wincing, made his way to the bars. He looked straight into Griffin's face. '*One* of the wounds? I only shot him but once! Took him low down in the left side. Might've cracked a couple of ribs, even a possibility it could've nicked one of his lungs, but I'm damn sure it wasn't a fatal wound.'

'No,' the lawman agreed, lighting his cigarette and blowing a plume of smoke into the cell through the bars. 'It was the one in his chest that finished him. Right through the heart.'

Connery frowned, held Griffin's gaze, then looked past the sheriff at Yuma. He shook his head slowly. 'I only shot him once – low down on the left side. That's gospel, Yuma.'

Shannon nodded. 'Well, that's what you told me earlier and I reckon I'd take Clay's word against that of three Mexicans who work for Vinnie Vincenz, Griff.'

89

Griffin held up a hand. 'I know Connery's a friend of yours, Yuma, but you stay outa this for now. I've had an official request from Marshal Tigge in Laredo to hold Connery on the charge of murderin' Brock and that's what I aim to do – I'll notify him, and he can send someone down to get him and take him back to Loredo, or he can arrange to hold the trial down here. But, as of now, Connery's my prisoner and he stays until Tigge decides what he wants to do.'

'I'll get you a lawyer, Clay,' Shannon offered.

Connery hesitated and then nodded: someone was framing him, and he reckoned it could only be Vinnie. The man did say to him that it would be a long, long time before he forgave Connery for throwing him down the stairs. He had always known Vinnie had a mean streak but he had never run afoul of it before. Came close a couple of times, but Vinnie always backed off.

This time, he was mean enough to follow through and nail Connery's hide to the wall.

But if Brock was dead, then his theory that it had been the freighter who had fired those shots at the first camp along the trail was wrong. But – Keller's mate from the riverboat had been with those bushwhacking bandits – *he* could have tried to shoot up the camp, on Keller's orders, later brought in the bandits for back-up at the cutting near the *laguna*.

But those bandits had come prepared to rip up the wagons, their tools in the waiting punt, so they must have been pretty sure the wagons carried whatever it was they were after.

And he sure wouldn't put it past Vinnie to have

loaded his contraband on board the Conestogas somehow, used those five boxes he had caught Brock loading as a decoy, inferring that *they* held the contraband, when it might already have been planted in the wagons before Connery showed up.

Only thing wrong with that theory was – *where? Where could Vinnie have put it?* The army had missed it and they had given the wagons a thorough going over. The only things they hadn't opened for inspection were the barrels of wine and tallow and pitch. De Witt had complained a whole damn Gatling gun could have been hidden in those barrels – and it was a possibility.

But that would mean Vinnie and Keller were likely in this together. No – *rivals!* That could be it. Vinnie wouldn't have bandits raid the wagons this side of the river if he was confident whatever he had hidden couldn't be found by the Customs.

But Keller – well, there had been rumours along the river for a long time that Keller was the man to see if you wanted any contraband smuggled across the border. Twice he had come under suspicion but each time the case hadn't stood up.

Maybe he was trying to steal Vinnie's contraband, whatever the hell it was. Somehow, Connery didn't think it was all that big. Yes, sure, a Gatling gun could be dismantled into its component parts, yet each part was still pretty big, so maybe they *had* been distributed amongst the casks after all. There were too many possibilities!

He realized the sheriff and Shannon were watching him as his mind churned with his theories. Hell, here he was trying to figure out how smugglers worked their trade and he had a damn *murder* charge hanging over him.

'Sheriff, I didn't kill Brock – I might've gotten my gun out first, but that was only because I was faster on the draw. He was going for his Colt when I shot him – *once!* Like I told you, low down on the left side. If he had a bullet in his ticker, someone else put it there.'

Griffin nodded slowly. 'Yeah, well, I dunno a helluva lot about you, Connery. I ain't had any trouble with you before this, but I've heard you can and do raise a bit of hell here and there along the river.'

'High spirits, Griff,' Shannon said quickly. 'Those long trading runs up and down river are just like a trail drive – boredom and routine set in. A man needs to cut loose now and again.'

'I've drove cows,' Griffin said shortly. 'I know all about cuttin' loose the curly wolf – but if a man breaks the law while he's doin' it, why, I'll lock him up and prosecute him just as far as I can go. And murder's about as bad a charge as any man can face.'

'It *is* as bad as it gets,' growled Shannon. 'Look, I'm gonna get Clay a lawyer and he'll want all the details.'

'OK, I'll bring Vincenz in here and he can make a full statement.'

Connery's hands grabbed the bars. 'Vinnie? He's here in Brownsville?'

'Sure – he came down on the *Blade* with Keller.'

Connery looked sharply at Shannon. 'Yuma, never mind the lawyer – get a bunch of men out to my wagons. *Armed* men with mules or ox, anything to bring 'em in as quick as you can. Vinnie's here for only one reason: to get his hands on whatever's hidden in those Conestogas!'

Shannon nodded and started out quickly. Griffin watched him go, blew smoke in Connery's face. 'I think you're wrong, Connery – I think Vinnie came down to see you hang.'

CHAPTER 8

RIOT

Connery had two visitors the next day. Not both together and neither welcome.

The first was Keller.

He came in limping, battered, bruised and bandaged, and he bared his teeth as he looked in through the bars. 'Where you belong at last, eh, Clay?'

'Swap you places any time, Kel.'

Keller's grin widened. 'Always the comeback, well, it won't save you this time.'

'You never know – then I'll claim compensation for what you did to my boat.'

Keller spread his bruised and swollen hands widely, all innocence. 'Me? I didn't do a thing – I was just manoeuvring the *Blade* and you happened to be in the way of my sternwheel wash. Too bad it put you up on those sandbanks, but you can hardly blame me, and as for someone burning it – well, I was up-river on my way to Del Rio when that happened.'

Connery was stretched out on the bunk, still digesting the greasy breakfast a Mexican girl had brought him earlier and pushed through the slot in the bars. He sat up now, swinging his legs over the side, took out tobacco and papers and began to build a cigarette, looking steadily at Keller.

'You must've made a quick turn-around to be back so soon.'

'Urgent cargo – and had some passengers to pick up in Laredo.'

'Including Vinnie Vincenz.'

'Yeah, he was one – man, he don't like you! He uses a stick now to get around, has these headaches and lapses of memory. Sawbones said it was concussion, caused by that fall down the stairs. Busted up a bit inside, too, they say. He's gonna dance on the gallows when they hoist you high, Clay.'

'Well, hope he falls off his walking stick.'

Keller laughed although it hurt his busted mouth to do so. He lifted a hand, pointed a forefinger and wriggled the thumb above it like a gun hammer. 'End of the line for you, Clay – I've waited a long time to see it. I'm even delaying landing, so I'll be here for your trial.'

Connery lit his cigarette, squinted through the smoke. 'You in on whatever it is Vinnie's smuggling?'

'Who me? I'm strictly a law-abiding riverboat captain. I don't go in for smuggling – King wouldn't stand for it. If there was even a suspicion of smuggling, he'd fire me like that.' He snapped thumb and forefinger but it hurt his aching hands and he swore under his breath.

Connery grinned. 'Thanks for dropping by, Kel.'

Keller scowled, turned to walk away down the passage. He paused and his ugly face was even uglier as he said through his broken teeth, 'Rot in hell, Clay! And rot *slow*!'

Connery smoked silently as the man left. *A bad enemy, Keller . . . very bad.*

Vinnie came limping in a couple of hours later, sallow and grey, drawn with pain, a bandage still around his head, leaning heavily on his walking stick and pressing one hand into his right side. His arm was out of the sling but Connery noticed how stiffly he moved it.

Breath hissed through his busted nose as he leaned on the stick at the bars, glaring in at Connery.

'Howdy, Vinnie, have a small accident?'

'I have a *big* accident, Captain – and I warned you that I would find it very hard to forgive you.' He bared his teeth, lips pulled back tightly. The stick wavered briefly in Cannery's direction. 'And here you are.'

'Totally innocent, Vinnie, as you well know.'

'But, Captain, you killed my man Brock! It was in cold blood and I have men who witnessed this. I felt it my duty to report everything to Marshal Tigge. After all, I am a law-abiding citizen of Laredo—'

'And I'm Salome of the Seven Veils! You're a vicious little son of a bitch, Vinnie. You put that extra bullet into Brock, paid off the doctor. I dunno how you got to Tigge, but he being the kind of man he is, he couldn't ignore Brock's death when you dressed it up the way you did. . . . And why didn't you let me get your contraband across the Rio and then make your move against me?'

'But Señor Brock had already died, Captain! I had to report it at once to the law – and I know nothing of any contraband. I am told the army at Rio Grande City thoroughly searched the wagons and found nothing illegal. Now that you are in jail on such a serious offence, the wagons still belonging to me, I felt I had to come down and see that they are still in good condition and, for old times sake, I will deliver your goods here and to Matamoroso.'

Connery had enough of the man's hypocrisy. 'Ah, get the hell out of here, Vinnie! You make me sick!'

'As you wish, Captain. I merely came to make my explanations. I am sorry you feel hostile towards me. If I can do anything to help, please ask . . . I will be in town for some little time yet.'

'Just don't come back here.'

Vinnie chuckled as he limped away. 'See you on the gallows, Captain!'

Connery swore softly and stretched out on his bunk again, smoking with savage motions.

Despite the unconcerned face he was putting on, he was mighty worried deep down – Vinnie had helped build his gallows high with his bought witnesses and lies.

As the thought came to Connery he unconsciously rubbed his throat. It felt dry and constricted.

As if with a tightening noose.

*

The third visitor came after supper. It was Yuma Shannon and he did not look any too happy.

'My men and the mule train are well on the way back to the wagons now, Clay, but the general talk around town is that you're for the high jump. Seems Vinnie has it all tied up neatly: he even brought those Mexican 'witnesses' down with him so there wouldn't be any delay, with signed depositions from Marshal Tigge. I spoke to a lawyer, a good man, and he'll take your case, but only at my insistence.'

'In other words, he doesn't think I have a hope, either.'

'That's it, I'm afraid – I don't know what else I can do.' He glanced briefly and casually towards the front-office door where the lanky deputy leaned, thumbs hooked in his gunbelt, his ear hanging out to catch their conversation.

'You're doing plenty, Yuma. Looks like I mightn't even get a chance to repay you.'

'You owe me nothing. You bought unlimited credit with me the night you hauled my family out of that fire and saved my neck, you know that, Clay.'

'Well, don't want you throwing good money after bad. If my case is hopeless, then so be it.'

Shannon frowned. 'That don't sound like you!'

'Ah, I was caught flat-footed in this – I ought've realized Vinnie would pull the rug out from under me for throwing him down the stairs in front of his woman.'

Shannon reached into his pocket and passed a slim carton of cigars through the bars. He glanced at the deputy who had stiffened slightly. 'Griff said it

98

was OK, Lew – you want to check the pack? Griff already did, but. . . .' He held out the thin cardboard box but the deputy hesitated, then shook his head, waved a bony hand.

Connery came across and took the packet. 'I'll ration 'em out.'

Shannon held on to the pack just a little longer than was necessary. Their gazes met through the iron. 'Have one after I leave – it'll help relax you.'

Connery frowned slightly but nodded.

Shannon sighed, shaking his head slowly. 'The lawyer'll come round in the morning. His name's Sheridan, handles most of my cattle-agency work. But he's a good man, knows his law. . . . I could send to Austin, maybe, for someone else if you want, but I think Sherry's as good as they come.'

'Obliged, Yuma. I'll settle for this Sheridan. Keller was here this morning. Can't quite figure where he fits into this. He was crowing, of course, and he's been trying to finish me off one way and another for a long time but there's something else here. I still think he might be either Vinnie's rival and after this contraband for himself, or else he's in partnership with him.'

'Where do you know Keller from, anyway?'

Connery smiled ruefully. 'He was one of the gamblers in the game where I won the *Rio Belle*. I didn't know at the time he was after the boat for himself. He was already working for King, but he needed that keelboat for some private deal. My guess is Mexes; it was ideal for that, with a good hold space and he could weave back and forth across the river a lot more easily and inconspicuously than a paddle-wheeler. Guess I ruined his plans. I know he was mixed up in some of that stuff – heard he got badly beaten because he had to welsh on a deal, maybe because he didn't have the keelboat.'

Shannon nodded. 'Yes – still a lot of trade in Mex labour. I'd heard that a couple of King's captains were involved but he fired two and I thought that was it – I hadn't heard Keller's name in relation to that.'

'He had to stop operations – that was why he needed a small boat like the *Belle*. Nearly sold it to him, but he got riled when I delayed, threatened me, so I decided I'd try the river trade myself, maybe make some quick money I could plough into my spread in Arizona.' He shrugged. 'And here I am – another scheme bites the dust and me with it.'

'Well, it's bad luck, all right, Clay. Anyway, relax with one of those cigars and I'll come back with Sheridan in the morning. Sleep well.'

Connery nodded. There was something strange about Shannon's words. They were innocuous enough, but his tone of voice seemed to be a little more light-hearted than was called for and, at the same time, the cattle agent's eyes seemed to be telling him something. . . .

Connery went back to his bunk, sat there a spell and reached for his tobacco sack and papers, aiming to roll a last cigarette as usual before trying to sleep. Then he changed his mind. The packet of cigars was on the bunk beside him and he decided he might as well smoke one of those. It just might relax him as Shannon said.

He had trouble pulling one cigar out of the packet of five, shook the packet until the ends protruded enough for him to grab. He tugged at them and realized that only four would come out freely. The fifth seemed a little fatter and was jammed against the side of the packet by the others.

He took out the four slim ones, then shook the fat one into his palm. The tobacco didn't look as neatly rolled as the others, seemed to have been disturbed. The outside leaf was loose and on impulse he broke the cigar in two.

A rolled-up piece of paper had been forced up into the cigar, which accounted for the tobacco's disturbance. There wasn't much light in the cell but enough for him to read the few words written inside the paper. All it said was:

There's going to be a high time in the old town tonight.
The noise'll probably keep you awake – I hope!

It didn't make sense to Connery. He thought about it for a while then dusted the destroyed tobacco leaf into the toilet bucket along with the torn-up note. He lit one of the other cigars and sat with his back against the wall, smoking – and thinking.

Only later did Sheriff Griffin realize that the men who started the riot all worked for Yuma Shannon in various capacities to do with his cattle business.

They were the labourers, the hard men who rode herd and rough trails, swung ropes and tackled mavericks and snorting bulls, castrated the males, bull-dogged the young ones for branding – and fought off Indians and rustlers along the trail.

They were just the kind of men to cut loose and paint the town red after Shannon's herds had been loaded on the riverboats or driven across to Matamoros for the drive down to the Hermoso Valley and the towns along Laguna Madre.

The ramrod was a man named Yancey, pushing fifty, a dried out looking *hombre* who rarely smiled, and then only in the company of perfumed women. He was a veteran of many fist fights and gun battles and had thousands of miles of dangerous trails behind him.

He was the kind of man who tore caps off beer bottles with his teeth, or, when in a hurry to assuage his thirst, broke the neck off a bottle and drank deeply, spitting out the broken glass from a bloodied mouth after the first few swallows.

He was sided by equally tough rannies when the whole bunch, ten in all, started out to reshape Brownsville.

There were two minor brawls in the Cockeyed Lady but they fizzled out quickly without much blood being spilled. It was too early in the night: nowhere near enough of the rotgut liquor had been consumed to drive the men berserk.

But they left a trail of increasing violence and damage behind as the night dragged on and they worked their way through the red light district but avoided crossing into Matamoros which was usually the haunt of carousing cowboys.

Shannon's orders had been plain enough: '*Yancey, you take the boys on a wing-ding, but you keep it this side of the river, savvy? No crossing into Matamorosa. Cut loose all you want, but* here *in Brownsville, and if you can kind of start some sort of riot around ten, ten-thirty so much the better – I'll pay all the bills.*'

So that was the way it had to be – and the way it was.

At ten minutes past ten in the smoke-fogged, noisy bar of the Sin Pit saloon, Yancey decided he wanted the company of a *señorita* in a red and orange dress who had already made three trips upstairs with other cowpokes.

Trouble was, a sailor from one of the riverboats was just smooging up to the *señorita*, tucking a folded bill down between her ample, sweat-gleaming breasts when Yancey strolled across, hitched at his gunbelt, sniffing through his narrow, bent nose as he announced, 'Rosita, *querida*, I been waitin' for you all night. I'm ready if you are, so let's be hightailin' up to your *boudoir*, huh?'

'Hey, you!' growled the sailor, a man much bigger than Yancey, younger, too, face slack with too much booze – and a growing anger tightening this slackness rapidly. 'Vamoose, pop! This one's mine, bought an' paid for – see?'

He indicated the folded money just showing in the woman's cleavage but Yancey didn't even look at it. He was smiling down into the *señorita's* face.

'Rosita, you 'member last time I was here and you said you'd show me some of that French lovin' you learned when you was in 'Frisco? You wanted a golden eagle before you'd do it – well, I got it right here and I'm eager to learn.'

He fumbled in a shirt pocket and gold glinted briefly. The woman pushed the sailor away, big white teeth flashing in Yancey's direction, but that was about as far as it went. The sailor grabbed the woman's shoulder, heaved her roughly out of her chair so that she squealed and sat down heavily on the filthy floor. Her screaming curses were lost in the general din, but by that time, the sailor was closing with Yancey, figuring to finish off this smaller man quickly and get back to Rosita. . . .

Nope – that wasn't the way it went. Yancey was suddenly no longer there in front of the sailor. Somehow he had stepped to one side and, as the sailor's big, knotted fists whistled through vacant air, Yancey drove two brutal, crippling blows into the man's kidney region.

The sailor groaned sickly and dropped to his knees, face grey and contorted as he tried to reach behind him to the place where it felt like someone had impaled him on a hot branding iron. Then Yancey's boot took him between the shoulders and he was thrust violently across the writhing *señorita* and—

After that no one was too sure just what happened. Except that some of the sailor's friends had witnessed what had happened to him and rushed Yancey in an avenging group.

The ramrod didn't have a huge chest but his bellow was stentorian and cut through the racket of drunken singing and arguments, even the sound of the tinny piano. These sounds were soon replaced by the racket of splintering furniture, the cussing of angry men, the howls of others who were hurt by fists or boots or broken bottles and chairs.

The cowboys rallied around Yancey – now bleeding from two cuts on his face, his shirt torn and dangling around his waist – and they formed a solid phalanx as an equally solid wall of riverboatmen lined up briefly before charging forward, snatching up chairs or bottles as they went.

Before long the entire bar room was involved, the drinkers who had stayed on the sidelines, enjoying this unexpected entertainment, suddenly finding themselves involved in arguments over who was winning or going to be the final winners – and before long, the first fist was thrown and someone staggered into someone else, who pushed back violently and then the blows rained down and men jumped on to the bar and those tables still standing, kicking out at brawling men, cracking heads. In seconds, they were hauled down off their high stands and soon tasted the stinking sawdust sprinkled over the floor so as to soak up spilled liquor – and blood.

There was plenty of blood and the brawls overflowed into the street, the bar room a shambles by this time. Other cowpokes from other trail herds were called upon to lend a hand – and more sailors came racing up from the docks.

Store windows shattered and doors were kicked in, goods looted, womenfolk terrorized.

By then, of course, Griffin and Lew and some other men hastily deputized had arrived and started firing off guns into the air and slowly the hostilities ceased and bloody, ragged men staggered to collapse on the edge of the boardwalks, or lurched to the horse trough where they sluiced bleeding, throbbing faces.

Griffin was savagely angry, bent his Colt barrel over several heads as men wanted to argue about being hauled off down to the jailhouse. He kicked half-conscious men to their feet, shoved and jostled them into a bunch watched over by Lew and his shotgun and those temporary deputies who weren't helping to drag in other captive brawlers.

There were a couple of brief foot chases through the alleys but the escapees were no match for uninjured deputies and soon the street outside the Sin Pit was crowded with moaning, bewildered men – bewildered, because half of them didn't even know how the hell they had become involved and now were nursing wounds and early hangovers, with the prospect of spending the night in a crowded jail to boot.

The saloon owner was poking and grabbing at Griffin, bemoaning the damage done to his establishment. The sheriff angrily slapped his hand away with his gun barrel and the saloon man withdrew it swiftly.

'Goddamn it, Griff! Go easy!'

'Get off my neck, Vern!' the sweating, harassed lawman growled. 'I got my hands full with this lot. Now I gotta get 'em down to jail before they decide to start up where they left off – and I dunno how I'm gonna fit 'em in. Looks like Connery's gonna have a lot of unwanted company tonight, but that's his hard luck.'

He raised his voice suddenly. 'All right, Lew, and you other deputies, start hazin' this lot down to the jail. I'll go on ahead and unlock the cells. . . .'

Still muttering, really pissed at a riot like this in his town, Sheriff Griffin stormed past the gawking townsfolk and went into his office through the open street door. He paused as he reached for the cell-block keys where they hung on the nail in the wall behind his desk. *Funny. He could've sworn he had closed the street door on the way out to the riot. . . .*

He reached down the keys and was sorting through them as he entered the passage to the cell block.

'Sorry, Connery, a murderer usually has a cell to hisself, but tonight you're gonna have a lot of company an' it ain't gonna be good. Drunks throwin' up, others moanin' about their sore ribs and. . . .' He stopped dead in his tracks. The door to Connery's cell stood open, the cell empty.

CHAPTER 9

SOUTHERN EXPOSURE

Connery breathed deeply of the night air down by the river, hearing the noise and bluster of the town in full swing far behind him now. It wasn't the first time he had been in jail but he had never – and could never – become accustomed to the confinement and the cloying, stale air of a prison cell that seemed heavy with the misery of past occupants.

Yuma Shannon had two horses waiting under some trees, held by a silent cowboy Connery guessed was one of Yuma's men. Things were moving mighty fast.

He had heard the riot start in town and knew exactly what Yuma's note in the fat cigar had meant: *Stay awake, be ready to move.*

With the street and saloon riots as decoys, Griffin storming down with all his deputies, it had been easy

108

for Shannon to slip into the law office, take down the cell keys and let Connery out. They had even gone out the front door of the office, Shannon hanging the keys back on their wall peg, and picking up Connery's sixgun and belt from a cupboard.

Most of the town were watching the riot and Griffin and his men breaking it up. No one saw the escaping prisoner and his rescuer as Yuma led the way out of town by side streets, coming out on the river bank, above the docks. The *Spanish Dancer* and *Blade* were at their moorings, lights burning as loading continued into the night – though all work had temporarily ceased as men ran to see the riot or even to join in against the marauding cowmen.

Now the silent cowboy under the trees led two horses out of the shadows, Shannon's Appaloosa and a black gelding for Connery. They mounted and Yuma spoke quietly to the cowboy who mounted his own horse and rode off towards town.

'Griffin likely knows I've gone by now,' Connery said quietly. 'He'll see that cowboy riding in from this way.'

'No. He knows to swing around and come in from the far side. When Griffin stops him, as he will, he'll say he saw a couple of horsemen racing for the bridge. Griff'll expect that, figure you'll cross the Rio to Matamoros by the quickest way. He'll likely have a man or two watching or guarding the bridge already.'

'So where do we go?'

'Across the river – but upstream.'

Connery held back as Shannon started to move off.

'C'mon, Clay!'

'You better not come, Yuma, you're involved deeply enough already.'

'C'mon!' was the cattle agent's only reply.

Connery heeled the black forward, feeling that there was a rifle in the scabbard, a bedroll, full canteen and saddle-bags. Shannon had planned well, the way he did most things.

The river crossing was easy enough, swimming the mounts, coming up on a long sandbar which they followed upstream a ways, where it swung in closer to the bank. The tide would wash out any tracks and it was easy enough to jump the horses over the last narrow strip of water – and land in Mexico.

'You're out of Griffin's reach now, Clay.'

'If he sees us, he'll shoot. He may not cross the border but he'll send a couple of bullets after me.'

Shannon chuckled. 'You *are* a pessimist at times!' But I guess you're right. Griff's a damn good lawman and takes his job seriously. He won't break any international laws but he'll set something in motion so as to get you back.' He sobered some then. 'Your escape does make it look as if you're guilty.'

'I'll take my chances, Yuma. This is just one more thing I owe you. Now don't start that business about the fire! Christ, it was long ago. I did what anyone would've done, so let me work up a debt to you – even if I can never fully pay it off.'

Shannon grinned crookedly, his features barely visible. 'They only made one of you, Clay! To hell with who owes what – we better get moving, we've a long way to go.'

Connery frowned. 'Where? I've got a couple of friends in Matamoros who'll hide me out.'

'I know a better place – in the Hermoso Valley.'

He spurred away before Connery could say anything and Clay shook his head as he urged the black after the cattle agent. The Hermoso Valley meant a twenty-mile ride.

Keller was beside himself with rage when he learned that Connery had escaped.

'Judas priest! How the hell could you go and leave your office unlocked – with the goddamn cell keys sittin' there for anyone who happened by!'

Griffin looked steadily at the man. 'I was in a hurry. That damn riot was tearin' up the town. And the local folk would be tearin' me up right now if I hadn't acted quickly. When property's bein' busted up by a bunch of drunken cowboys and riverboatmen, you don't care about minor things like leavin' an office unattended – you *act*!'

Keller swore. 'Well, damn it, Griff! What the hell're you doin' about Connery?'

'I've notified the Mexican *Rurales* chief and their border patrol. They'll be watchin' for him. They'll hold him on some pretext or other until I can organize extradition papers. But I've told 'em if he puts up a fight, to shoot back – and shoot to kill if they have to.'

'Christ, what a mess!'

'Keller, you close that mouth of yours before I find some reason to toss you in jail.' Griffin had had enough criticism and his face was flushed, his jaw

111

jutting, and his hand ready to draw his gun.

Keller calmed down, or at least made a show of doing so, though he was in turmoil inside. 'You told Vinnie?'

'He knows, Now I've told you, out of courtesy. Just leave things to me and I'll have Connery back here pretty soon.'

'It was Shannon, wasn't it? It had to be him busted him out. Hell, likely he even arranged the brawl, knowin' how you'd come down on it, leave him a chance to get Connery out of the cell.'

Griffin's face gave nothing away. 'That's one theory I'm workin' on, but *how* it happened ain't as important as gettin' Connery back – and like I said, Kel, you leave this to me. You poke your nose in and it'll get tweaked – hard.'

Keller watched the sheriff leave and he sat for a while in his room, sipping a good quality brandy. Then he heaved out of his chair, grabbed his hat, buckled on a gunbelt and went out into the night.

He found Vinnie in a suite of rooms at the Hotel Durango on Descanso Street. The Mexican freighter did not look to be a happy man, had his game leg up on a cushion while a young Mexican woman massaged it expertly. Vinnie waved her away irritably as a gunhung *gringo* named Borden showed Keller in. A sign from Vinnie and Borden, the replacement for Brock, folded his arms and leaned against the closed door. He was tall, hard-muscled, cold-eyed.

'You have heard, of course,' Vinnie said.

'Whole blame town's heard by now! That damn

Shannon! We'd've had Connery long since if he hadn't bought in.'

Vinnie made a loose kind of movement with his good hand. 'I had forgotten that Shannon was beholden to Connery. It has prolonged things, that is all. The deal will proceed.' Vinnie's bruised face hardened. 'Your bandits failed to take the goods, Keller. Normally, I would have you killed, but I think now the only way is for us to become partners.'

Keller smiled crookedly. 'Just what I had in mind. I wasn't tryin' to steal your stuff because I have anythin' against you, Vinnie – I saw the chance to kill Connery, have him die in a raid by Mex *bandidos*, and if I could make a profit at the same time, well. . . .' He shrugged.

Vinnie's face was still hard. 'Brock was your man, wasn't he? He told you about the goods being hidden in that Conestoga?'

Keller shrugged. 'Well, he passed on information to me from time to time.'

'Which explains why some of my deals went wrong – and I lost my goods – but no doubt you lined your pockets at my expense.'

Keller stood up and went to a table where there were bottles and glasses. He poured himself a whiskey without invitation, ignoring the obvious stirring of Borden. But Vinnie waved Borden back and told Keller to pour him a drink, too.

Keller handed it to him, sipped his own, looking at Vinnie over the rim of the glass. 'We should've gotten together long before this, Vinnie. The *Blade* is just cryin' out to be used for somethin' other than the legit trade that King wants it for. . . . No hard feel-ings?'

'I have not yet decided. But for now, we must work together. You know that Shannon has sent men and a mule team to bring in those wagons?' Keller nodded. 'They will arrive tomorrow or the next day. I have arranged things with the Customs on both sides of the river for them to be passed through, but we will need someone to drive them to their – desti-nation.'

He looked closely at Keller who smiled crookedly. 'You mean to – Salvadore?'

Vinnie's eyes narrowed. 'So! I suspected someone was making enquiries into my business! But not Brock, not until he was raving in pain with his wound. But he paid for his treachery, and gave me a weapon to use against Connery.'

Keller's smile widened, even though it hurt his smashed mouth. 'Connery should never've thrown you down those stairs, should he? How'd you get around Tigge?'

'He was lured out of town on a rustling pretext, headed a posse up into the hills. It would've been days before he returned, and by then, I was down here, making my own arrangements.' He drank some whiskey. 'Salvadore will be expecting a *gringo* to bring in the wagons – I was going to send Borden, but you must have some men to call upon, eh?'

It didn't take Keller long to decide there was a man who could do the job. 'Feller named Whiskey Jack Clute ought to fit the bill.'

Vinnie straightened painfully in his chair, frowning. 'With a name like that he hardly sounds reliable!'

Keller laughed. 'Oh, he's not named because he boozes a lot – it's because he used to make moonshine – had a problem with Connery sometime back. Tried to ship some of it on the *Rio Belle* on the quiet. Somethin' like when you had Brock load them decoy boxes. Connery didn't like that. Clute can still only chew on one side of his mouth. Connery's gunsight smashed up all the teeth on the other side – and Clute's never forgotten it.'

That, at last, made Vinnie Vincenz smile.

He raised his glass. 'Then let us drink to Señor Whiskey Clute – long may his hate abide within him!'

Sun-up promised a sweltering day, heat-haze rising from the trail ahead already. The usual early morning coolness was missing as the two riders put their weary mounts down the high trail from the rim of a ravine.

Both men were saddle-weary and the horses showed signs of the long night ride down from the Rio. They rode through the ravine, keeping to the shadows where it was cooler, stopped for a quick breakfast of coffee and beans by a shallow stream.

They hadn't spoken much during the ride, too tired for one thing, busy with their thoughts for another.

'How much further, Yuma?' Connery asked, taking out one of the cigars Shannon had given him in the jail, offering the crushed cardboard pack to the cattle agent.

Shannon took one and they lit up. 'A few more miles – but I will leave you at the trail fork, and go back to Matamoros.'

Connery looked at him sharply. 'And where do I go?'

Yuma gestured with the burning cigar, down the ravine. Connery could see plains country and distant hills blurred by a bluish haze beyond the rocky walls.

'To the valley. You will come to a sign that points the way to Hacienda Renaldo.' Yuma drew deeply on the cigar, mouthed the smoke while watching Connery's face. 'Glenda's there. She's governess to Don Renaldo's children. His wife died and—'

'Now wait a minute! I don't expect your daughter to hide me out – specially if she only works for this Don Renaldo! You can't ask her to take that risk, Yuma.'

'She will do it gladly for you.' Shannon smiled. 'You don't remember how she worshipped you, Clay?'

'Ah, hell, she was just a kid and she saw me as a – a—'

'As a hero,' cut in Yuma. 'Which you were – and are – to her. She is still very young but – well, you wait and see. The years have been kind to her. As for Don Renaldo, well, he is an old and good friend.' He reached into his jacket pocket and handed Connery a creased envelope. 'There are two short letters in there, one for Glenda, one for Rennie – Don Renaldo. You will be safe there, Clay. I'll be in touch and keep you up to date with what's happening.'

Connery didn't say anything as he put the envelope in his pocket. *He would never be able to repay this man for all he was doing for him.*

There was little use in mentioning yet again what a debt he owed him, but Connery wasn't a man who could simply sit back and let others take care of him.

'Yuma, make sure Mac and Ruben don't get into any trouble. If you can, tear those wagons apart, literally, see just what the hell it is Vinnie's got hidden in them.'

Shannon hesitated. 'You're still sure there is something? Even after the army's thorough search?'

'Has to be. Those bandits were after it and the army never found it. If it's not in the casks, it must be in the wagons, and that means *in* them.'

'How. . . ?'

'Those are original Pennsylvania Conestogas. The planks and frames are mighty heavy hardwood. The wagon-bed ones are three or four inches thick – I figure some of them have been hollowed out and whatever Vinnie's smuggling has been hidden inside.'

'Surely the army would've noticed?'

Connery shook his head. 'Maybe not. You've seen some of that Mexican woodwork on their boxes with secret compartments for the ladies to keep their diaries and jewels in. Their inlaying and joints are perfect, almost invisible in polished wood – it wouldn't be too hard to cover any joins on weathered grey hardwood planks if you had the right men.'

Shannon nodded slowly. 'All right – I'll tell the Customs.'

'No, Yuma. Vinnie will have it fixed already. When

117

Rube and Mac bring in the wagons, go to work on them before they try to take them through Customs and across the river into Mexico.'

'And if we find anything?'

Connery gave it a little thought. 'Maybe you could tell Griffin.'

'Griffin!'

'He seems the type who'd be interested in exposing crooked Customs men – all he has to do is watch and see which ones give the wagons the OK without a real search. Might be a problem proving Vinnie put whatever it is there in the first place, but just finding it will mess up his plans plenty.'

Shannon looked at Connery carefully.

'Then he'll come after you.'

Connery smiled. 'I'll be waiting.'

There was no mistaking Hacienda Renaldo.

There was a wide, high archway in white-painted adobe with a large sign swinging from tarred chains that were showing a few streaks of rust. The name was carved deeply into a weathered timber plank.

And there were two armed Mexicans waiting in the shade of persimmon trees well within view of the gateway. They rode out to meet Connery as he came down the dusty trail, the black looking almost grey now, except for the deep, dark rivulets of sweat streaking his coat.

'*Alto, amigo!*' called the fat guard, showing crossed bullet belts across his chest and two guns on his thighs. The fact that he didn't have a weapon in his hand showed he was quite confident he could reach

118

one quickly if necessary.

Besides, the second guard, a slim Mexican, held a Winchester carbine across his thighs, one hand on the action, a finger already through the trigger guard.

Connery hauled rein and lifted a hand in greeting.

'*Hola, amigos!* You speak English?'

'Yes.' The fat one gestured to the sign. 'You read Spanish?'

'I can see this is the *hacienda* of Don Renaldo. Which is where I am going.'

The fat man grinned. 'You are here, but perhaps this is as far as you go, eh?'

The slim man moved the rifle suggestively.

'Well, I'd like to speak with Don Renaldo.' Connery moved his hand slowly, patting his shirt pocket. 'I have a letter for him – and for Señorita Glenda Shannon.'

The Mexicans exchanged a quick glance.

'Glenda, the *institutriz?*'

Connery nodded. 'From her father, Señor Shannon.'

'Ah! You will ride ahead slowly, *señor*, and follow my directions – you will not dismount until you are told. *Comprende?*'

'*Comprende – compadre.*'

But Connery's little joke did not bring any smiles to the guards' faces and they motioned him through the archway, telling him again to walk the black ahead of them towards the distant low white building on the rise, some half mile distant.

When they arrived, another armed guard

appeared from a patio on one side and the slim gate guard turned his mount and rode swiftly back to his position. The fat man spoke rapidly in Spanish and the house guard's call brought a servant woman to the big ornately carved wooden door.

A brief explanation, with Glenda's name mentioned, and minutes later, Connery stood in a cool, spacious room with tiled floor and a magnificent view out across the valley.

He waited, aware of his dishevelled condition, and then he heard some kind of small disturbance beyond the doors, a raised voice, the rapid clicking of heels on the tiles. And then the door crashed open and something with colour swirling around it hurtled towards him and next instant there was a pair of slim brown arms around his neck, a wave of perfume, and then warm, moist lips pressed against one corner of his mouth.

He staggered and managed to keep his balance, instinctively reaching out with both hands and finding a slim waist in his grip as he tried to see through a swirl of dark-brown hair.

'Clay! Oh, Clay, how wonderful to see you!'

He kept his hands on the slender hips and managed to step back a little, looking into the flushed, excited face of a young girl in her late teens – no! a young *woman*, beginning to blossom.

He smiled. 'Just as well you recognized me, Glenda – I doubt I would've known you! Why – you're beautiful!'

She laughed, a sweet sound in his dusty ears. She

punched him lightly in the ribs. 'You mean I wasn't beautiful before?'

'No! Hell, no – I didn't mean – that! I—' He stopped floundering when he saw the laughter in her dark eyes and another welcoming smile. The pert little nose was slightly turned up at the end as he remembered, but the rest of her – the swell and curve of the breasts, the slender waist, the brown legs showing beneath the short, brightly coloured Spanish skirt – well, those things were different to the last time he had seen her.

Then a man's voice spoke behind him.'Ah, *señor*, I see you have renewed acquaintance with my little *cervato* – and such an agile little fawn, no? Welcome to my *hacienda*.'

Connery turned, Glenda still clinging smilingly to his right arm, and had his first look at Don Renaldo.

The man was in a wheelchair.

CHAPTER 10

CONTRABANDISTAS

Shannon tangled with Griffin over the jail break as expected but Yuma was well-used to handling hard-nosed lawmen or businessmen, and he shrugged off Griffin's raw accusations.

'Griff, I've known you a long time – you're a good lawman and you're stubborn and persistent. But drop this foolishness – I told you I was visiting friends across in Matamoros at the time of the riots and if anyone thought they saw me this side of the river at that time, *they were mistaken.*'

Griffin gave Shannon a long, hard contemplative look. He nodded gently. 'I won't bother askin' for the friend's name, Yuma – which doesn't mean I believe you. Only that I'm sure the friend you nominate will back your story.'

Shannon smiled crookedly. 'I guess that's about as tactful as you can get, Griff, so we leave it at that, right?'

'For now – I'd appreciate it if you let me know if you're gonna leave town – and where you're goin'.'

'Now I know that's not an order, because you don't really have the authority to enforce it. . . .'

Griffin coloured slightly. 'A request then.'

'Sure – fair enough. Matter of fact I'm on my way out of town right now . . . to meet the wagons that my men are escorting into town – OK?'

'Like to see them wagons come in myself.'

Tightlipped, Griffin swung away and Shannon climbed into the saddle of a fresh horse: his weary Appaloosa was being groomed and fed by the Brownsville Livery.

He spurred away, anxious to meet the wagons.

They were still over a mile out when Shannon saw the small cavalcade, the armed men he had sent to escort the wagons strung out, riding military fashion, rifle butts on thighs, heads up and alert. The big wagons lumbered and swayed as the mule teams struggled to pull them towards town. Two men were walking beside the team of the lead wagon and he recognized Ruben first by his skin colour and then McAllen's squat form.

Shannon's man in charge, Lute Merryman, rode up and touched a hand to his hat brim.

'Mornin', Mr Shannon. We're kinda late, but them mules sure don't like haulin' somethin' as heavy as them wagons. No trouble along the way – though I think we were watched. Caught a couple flashes that might've been sun-hit lenses in the hills.'

'Thanks, Lute. See the boys have a couple of

drinks on me when they get to town.'

McAllen walked the horse alongside. He brought them up to date on what had been happening, noting the look the men exchanged when he told them where Connery was holed-up.

'Did you have any luck looking for contraband?' Shannon asked.

Neither man spoke right away. Then Ruben cleared his throat and said, 'We best leave that till we see the skipper, Mr Shannon.'

'If you found anything, he wants it put back in its hiding place and then taken through Customs across the river.'

'The hell for?' demanded McAllen, in his usual truculent manner.

'He wants Sheriff Griffin told about it and then he'll watch and see which Customs officers pass it through – get a notion who's been bribed.'

'And if we're caught with it?' McAllen snapped. 'We're the suckers, ain't we?'

'No. That's the idea of telling the sheriff first. He can vouch he knew about it and it was a set-up to bring the bribed Customs men out into the open.'

McAllen frowned. 'What you think, Rube?'

'I think we know how highly the skipper thinks of Mr Shannon here, so I reckon we take his word as gospel, Mac.'

It didn't please McAllen, but he saw the sense of it and said, 'Well, we did finally locate the hidin' place. Like you said the cap'n figured, some of the planks in the wagon bed had been hollowed out for three or four feet, the "lid" was lined with sheet iron so it wouldn't ring hollow if anyone tapped it. Damn fine work.'

'It fits back so well it was even hard gettin' a knife blade into the openin',' Ruben told Yuma.

Shannon was alert now, lowered his voice. 'And what was hidden in there? Guns? Dismantled ones, I mean.'

'No guns, Mr Shannon. But these were *parts* of guns all wrapped up in greased paper.' Ruben raised his eyes to Shannon's face. 'I did a short spell in the army once. They trained us how to use a Gatling gun, but we never did get to use one in action. What we found were parts for a Gatling gun.'

'Yeah,' snapped McAllen, impatient as usual. 'Gears for the handle that rotates the barrels, breech covers and cartridge extractors, even magazine and hopper clips.'

'No Gatling gun can fire without these parts bein' fitted,' Ruben dropped in. 'There were enough for sixteen guns – or could be for eight guns, with spares.'

'And eight Gatling guns were stolen in that raid on the San Antone to Corpus Christi train. . . .' Shannon sounded thoughtful, then smiled thinly. 'Be just like Vinnie to be in on the deal, hand over the guns to whoever wanted 'em, but hold back the essential parts. They'd bring a lot more than the guns themselves in the end. He could name his price.'

'We ain't told no one,' McAllen said. 'Not even De Witt – we did it on the quiet while we were waitin' for the new teams to arrive.'

125

'Well, gentlemen, I don't think we'll tell *anyone* about this after all,' Shannon said. 'We keep it just between the three of us – agreed?'

Ruben and Mac just stared at him.

A horse had rolled on Don Renaldo, crippling his legs, crushing nerves and tendons so that they would never work again.

'I used to breed fine horses, with an Arab strain, Señor Connery, for El Presidente's personal cavalry – so you can understand how the news that I would never walk – or ride – again affected me. Much worse even than the news that the President was taking over my stables – for which I still have to be recompensed.'

The Mexican ranchero didn't sound all that bitter so Connery guessed he had come to terms with it long ago. He was a man who had once been tall but was now hunched over from being so long in a wheelchair. There was grey in his black hair, quite a deal of it, and also just beginning to show in the bushy moustache under his eagle nose. His eyes were bright and dark and always grew soft when he looked in Glenda's direction.

'My wife was very understanding, but she died giving birth to our second child.' Don Renaldo smiled at Glenda. 'Now the beautiful daughter of my good friend Yuma Shannon has come to care for my children – you will meet them later. Two wonderful little girls who I am certain will melt your heart.' He suddenly clapped his hands. 'But, I chatter on and boast too much about my family!'

'As any proud parent would, Rennie,' Glenda said, smiling. She glanced towards Connery. 'He has every right to boast about his daughters, Clay!'

'I'm sure he has,' Connery said, feeling a little out of his depth here. 'I'm grateful to you for allowing me to stay here a while. Don Renaldo—'

'Please – call me Rennie. . . .'

'OK, Rennie, I won't stay any longer than I have to. I don't want to put you in any danger.'

Renaldo threw up his hands. 'Danger? Why, *señor*, we live with constant danger here. Do you not know that the hills behind this house are crawling with *rebeldes*? And not just rabble who hide behind the name of *revolutionarios*. We are graced with the presence of El Salvadore himself.'

Connery arched his eyebrows, glanced at Glenda, but she didn't seem perturbed in any way. The man calling himself 'Salvadore', the Saviour, was widely known and popular throughout Mexico – the man was a living legend. As Renaldo had said, he was no mere upstart. This man was educated, had travelled extensively throughout the country and built up a massive following. . . . El Presidente and his corrupt government were said to be very worried about Salvadore, and had put a big bounty on his head There were other rebels, too, most just plain thieves and brigands, using the 'rebel' tag as a cover to commit crimes.

But not the men who followed Salvadore – theirs was a more subtle kind of resistance. They used words to preach insurrection, mainly of a passive sort – by avoiding or refusing to pay the unfair and exor-

127

bitant taxes imposed upon all and sundry, but favouring the richer classes; quietly slowing military columns by sabotaging the trails, using avalanches, or blocking a narrow pass with rambling herds of sheep or slow-moving cattle (in their hundreds), or tying-up supplies to government troops, the driver and engineer abandoning military freight trains in the middle of nowhere, joining men who were waiting with fast horses; or even by removing lengths of rail track on bridges. It was resistance without violent confrontation. Salvadore's men were placed in strategic positions in government offices, too, and saw that paperwork became disorderly and chaotic because of 'mistakes' and delays. All calculated to harass El Presidente.

Salvadore was never short of followers: men saw in him true salvation from the oppressive regime they had endured for so many years. They waited for the big day when the full-scale uprising would happen – long overdue, it was inevitable, and then there would be guns and violence.

'You may meet El Salvadore himself, *señor*,' Don Renaldo said slowly, watching Connery closely. 'It has been known for him to come to dinner here at the *hacienda*.'

Connery saw the exchange of looks between the *ranchero* and the girl, but he couldn't read anything into it.

'He even stores some of his – goods – on my *rancho*.'

'You are a man who believes in taking risks, Rennie,' he said quietly, knowing that Renaldo was feeling him out: for what he wasn't sure. 'If El Presidente got to hear about that, I'd hate to think what might happen.'

Renaldo smiled and spread his hands.'But why would he suspect me? I am one of the nobility, the favoured ones. Why should he even think I might be involved with someone such as Salvadore?'

Connery frowned. Renaldo sounded almost flippant – as if he was enjoying some private joke.

The Customs made a thorough search of the Conestoga wagons – on both sides of the river – but neither the American or Mexican officers located the contraband. There was no sign that they were not doing their job properly and this puzzled Mac and Ruben – and Shannon who had found an excuse to stay close to the crossing station. As the wagons rumbled out into Matamoros, he rode forward to meet with Ruben and McAllen.

'Well, that was a fizzer. Those men seemed to be doing their jobs properly.'

'Could've been practice,' McAllen said heavily. 'If they been takin' bribes for years – and my bet is they have – they'd have a routine worked out by now that makes it look like they're doin' their job thoroughly.'

Ruben nodded agreement and Shannon, frowning a little, agreed. 'And where are the first deliveries to be made?' he asked.

Ruben brought out his newly stamped manifests and rattled off a couple of addresses in Matamoros itself. 'Then we got two out on the coast, small villages, and the rest go to the Hermoso Valley. One or two *ranchos* there, mostly barrels of pitch and American canned food.'

Shannon nodded. 'Does Clay normally bring these things down himself?'

'No, we off-load at Brownsville. But he's late this time what with the wreck of the *Belle* and one thing and another. You know him – hates to bust a schedule and keep folk waitin'. He knows they'll be lookin' for their stuff, so we bring it down by wagon. Only done it once before so we're not too familar with the trails.'

'I know this part of the country pretty well, and the Hermoso – what part of the valley?'

'Dunno. Just got the names of the *ranchos.* . . .' Ruban consulted his papers again. 'Place called Miraflores.'

'Yeah, I know that – acres of gardens under irrigation. Restful on the eyes.'

'San Hilario in the north, I think . . .'

'I've heard of it, but haven't been there.'

'. . . and Rancho Renaldo. . . .'

Ruben let his voice trail away as he saw the shock hit Shannon like a fist to the belly.

Connery was on the side patio, smoking after breakfast, when he noticed riders gathering in the courtyard. Armed men, and the man in charge seemed to be the fat guard from the gate. He was called Vibora which Connery knew meant snake, but not just an ordinary snake – it was the most poisonous kind.

Now he could see that the man bore absolutely no resemblance to a reptile in shape so he must have earned the name for other reasons. Perhaps because he was snake-quick with a gun. And deadly, too. . . .

He asked Glenda about the armed men when she came out on to the patio after tending to Don Renaldo's children.

'They go to meet the wagons,' she told him and, at his quick look, 'Of course! This time they are your wagons, Clay, we expect them this afternoon.'

'Good. Does Rennie usually send an armed escort?'

The girl hesitated, then shook her head. 'Only once before – when he was expecting something special. There are rebels other than Salvadore in those hills and they sometimes raid the wagons coming down from the States.'

Connery nodded, hitched at his gunbelt. 'Think I'll ride along.'

'You should get Rennie's permission,' she said quickly, adding, 'He is a stickler for tradition – and he is, after all, the *ranchero*.'

'Yeah – OK.'

Don Renaldo seemed a little surprised, but gave Connery permission to ride along – he would have gone in any case, but he figured it best to keep in good with Rennie. The man was powerful and highly respected in the district. He had learned that much in the few days he had been here.

As he readied to ride, the girl placed a hand on his arm. 'Clay, be careful. I hear that Rennie is expecting a raid this time. I'm not sure why but – there is a bandit called Carnicero, the butcher, whose territory the wagons have to pass through. He is ruthless.

Rarely anyone survives his raids.'

'Thanks for the warning.' Connery still hesitated, one boot in the stirrup. 'Has this Salvadore ever visited since you've been here?'

She lowered her eyes, 'I've never been introduced if he has. Rennie has plenty of visitors for dinner and I am not always included. They are old friends of his. From *ranchos* in the valley, I think. Why do you ask, Clay?'

He shook his head and swung into the saddle, smiling. 'Just curious. Thought I might like to meet Salvadore himself. I've been hearing about him for years.'

He rode to the courtyard where Vibora waited with his armed men.

'*Bienvenida, señor,*' the Mexican greeted him. 'You will place yourself at my orders?'

Connery nodded. 'Unless there's a fight – then I figure it'll be every man for himself.'

The Mexican nodded. '*Sí,* that will most certainly be the case if we meet Carnicero!'

And meet the *bandido* they did. With twenty men armed to the teeth and out for slaughter and theft.

They were four hours' ride out from the *rancho* when the dust raised by the wagons was sighted. The lumbering Conestogas were coming through a wide pass which seemed safe enough from ambush because the walls sloped so gradually and there was plenty of open space.

But the Butcher knew his territory and he had men placed in several positions where they were hidden by rocks. They allowed the wagons to work through most of the pass and where it narrowed in a short bottleneck before opening out on to the plains, they struck.

Ruben and McAllen were handling the teams by reins now, for the wagons' loads had been lightened considerably after Brownsville and deliveries to Matamoros and the villages on the coast. A twenty-mule team pulled each wagon now and although the animals misbehaved out of pure cussedness, the haul was not as hard as previously.

But they were animals who did not answer well to long reins, even if a man walked at their head, like the slim Mexican youths they had brought with them from Brownsville.

At the first sign of the bandits rushing out of their hiding places, McAllen stood up on the seat, levering a shell into his rifle's breech, shouting at the youths to use their whips and get the goddamned jugheads *moving!*

He threw his rifle to his shoulder and started shooting as fast as he could work lever and trigger. One of the hard-riding bandits lurched in the saddle but did not fall. The other shots flicked dust from around the galloping feet of the horses whose flanks were red with blood from guthook spurs.

Mac staggered and stepped over the seat back into the wagon bed, hunkering down amongst some of the freight, supporting the rifle on the backrest. Ruben shouted and cussed the mules, lashing with the long reins, while the frightened Mexican youths cracked their whips but obviously wanted to get out of there fast.

'Hell! There must be a coupla dozen of the sonuvers!' shouted McAllen, but Ruben didn't answer, concentrating on getting the heavy wagon moving.

But the vehicles were far too heavy to speed away in a chase and the bandits spread out around them, picking off some of the mules in both teams. The animals went down squealing and kicking, the others behind and in front being pulled off-balance, reins tangling.

Carnicero's men were well experienced at such raids, stayed back, hunting cover, letting the wagons slide to a stop. Ruben and Mac were both in the bed of their wagon, rifles shooting whenever they saw bandits moving. One of the youths had been hit and lay sprawled in the dust. The other cowered beneath the wagon. The drivers of the other Conestoga, Mexicans hired by Shannon, were crouching down behind the heavy boards, ducking quickly as the bullets splintered the wood: they had not been hired to fight.

Shannon himself had been dozing in the back of that wagon and he unshipped his rifle now, pushed the barrel under the loose canvas of the awning and searched for targets.

The bandits were content, it seemed, just to pick off more of the mules, their bullets shredding the canvas awnings, chipping away at the wooden sides. They had crippled the wagons and would play with them until they were ready for the final slaughter.

But they had not counted on Don Renaldo's men.

CHAPTER 11

BANDITS & REBELS

They swept in, riding in an arc, Vibora in the lead with Connery alongside. They had held their fire and were almost upon the holed-up *bandidos* before any of them noticed.

At a hand signal from Vibora, the *vaqueros* opened fire and a hail of lead raked the hiding places of Carnicero's men. Bullets screamed from rocks and the shale walls behind the bandits, ricocheting downwards and flattening before slashing like deadly sabres. The cries of the bandits were lost in the hammering of the guns and the whining ricochets.

These were hard men, living wild, used to plundering for their requirements, knowing that if they didn't fight for what they wanted, then the rewards would be nothing – or death. So, even as four men fell, either badly wounded or killed, the rest ducked down and when opportunity offered, rose and snapped shots at the charging *vaqueros*.

Connery felt the air-whip of a slug passing his face, instinctively ducked, lying along his mount's back, the flying mane whipping at his eyes and momentarily blinding him.

When he could see properly again he found he was in amongst the bandits. His mount was lifting over a low rock and Connery glimpsed a Mexican rolling on to his back so as to shoot up at him. He thrust the rifle down one-handed and triggered, saw the man slammed back, his face just a splash of red. Then he almost fell from the saddle, snatched at the horn and would have been all right except the horse swerved to avoid another boulder.

Connery spilled from the saddle, clutched the rifle close to his body as he hit in a shower of dust, rolling and floundering. He came to an abrupt halt against a startled bandit and shoved the rifle at him, remembering he hadn't yet had time to lever in a fresh shell. But the rifle barrel took the man in the mouth and he choked on shattered teeth and blood gushing from torn tongue and lips. He wrenched his head away and gave Connery time to jack in a fresh load. The bullet finished the Mexican instantly, taking him through an eye socket.

Connery spun away, rolling up to his knees, levering again, finding there were no more shells in the magazine. He thrust the gun aside, saw a man swinging a smoking rifle on him and palmed up his sixgun even as he threw himself backwards. The man shuddered as two slugs exploded in his chest and then Connery was frantically spinning aside as a big man came hurtling bodily at him.

The freighter tried to dodge, but the man's arms were spread like wings and a hot sixgun took him across the side of the head. Lights blazed and whirled and one leg folded under him. He lurched aside as a fist swung at him. It grazed his jaw but knocked him to one side so that the man's swinging boot missed. Connery fired his Colt and the big man staggered, grunted, then bared his teeth and lunged forward again, knocking Connery's gun hand aside.

Clay smelled the foul breath, turned his buzzing head away from the spray of spittle, hooked upwards and back with an elbow. It was a lucky blow, took the big man in the throat and he went rigid, clawing at his neck. Connery smashed the top of his head into the contorted face, got his gun into position and rammed the muzzle up under the man's arm. It triggered with a muffled sound and jarred wildly against his wrist as the man fell away.

A bullet clipped his shirt sleeve and the tug was hard enough to send him staggering – he twisted but was still moving, and stumbled. A Mexican with a fresh bullet burn across his face, was using the bolt action of his rifle awkwardly as Connery's outflung arm struck a rock and the sixgun fell from his grip. The bandit bared yellowed teeth as he lifted the rifle, sure of the killing shot now.

Then his head seemed to explode in a mist of pink and grey and white splintered bone as he was driven over the rock. Connery jerked his head around and saw the fat Vibora hauling rein, his smoking gun aimed down – but there was no need for a second shot.

Ears ringing, Connery picked up his Colt and got to his feet a little groggily, waved at the Mexican *segundo* but the man was past, spinning his mount, pistol seeking new targets. There were only scattered shots now and Connery suddenly realized they were finishing shots – the surviving *vaqueros* were moving amongst the bandits, killing those who had survived. All had been wounded but whether just slightly or more seriously it earned them a fatal bullet.

He coughed in the thick cloud of dust and hanging gunsmoke as Vibora put his mount across to where Connery stood, reloading his pistol. 'So ends the butcher's career,' the Mexican said, indicating the man whose head he had literally blown off.

'I'm obliged, Vibora.'

The Mexican shrugged. 'You must see to your friends.'

Mac had been wounded, twice. Once in the head, a mere shallow groove across the scalp, and again in the right arm. Ruben was tending to him when Connery came to their wagon.

'Howdy, boys. You gonna survive, Mac?'

'I better – you still owe me wages.'

Connery grinned, 'Yeah, you'll make it all right. How about you, Rube?'

He made a show of looking himself up and down, spread his arms. 'Seem to be as perfect a specimen of manhood as ever – just lucky I guess. Or the gals I ain't met yet are.'

Connery punched him lightly on the shoulder, and Ruben told him about the Customs. Clay was still puzzling over it when Shannon came up, blood splashed on his clothes.

'Damn! Two of those young Mex boys we hired to walk ahead of the mules are dead. Howdy, Clay. Everything OK at the *hacienda*?'

'Sure – Glenda's fine and so is Rennie. Rube says you never told Griffin about finding the contraband.'

Shannon shook his head, searching in his pocket for a cigar. 'It hit me of a sudden that Griff was in a perfect position for a *contrabandista* – reputation as a strict lawman, knowing all the Customs men, able to walk or ride over the border when and as he pleased – and what's more, take friends with him or vouch for them so they weren't searched as thoroughly as they would be ordinarily.'

'Griffin?' asked Connery. 'But he's respected as the toughest lawman ever to hit our side of the Rio since Wild Bill Hicock turned in his badge.' Shannon merely looked at him with a sort of expectant expression and slowly Connery nodded. 'Yeah – just as you said. Above suspicion, and in the perfect place to run contraband ... but there's no proof, Yuma.'

'No, unless we can get a look at his bank balance. I'll bet it's a helluva lot more than he could've saved out of his wages.'

'Means he'd have to be tied in with Vinnie – and Keller.'

'Yeah – I checked with the Brownsville telegraph office. Griff never got any wire from Marshal Tigge in Laredo about Brock dyin'. He arrested you because Vinnie asked him to, in person. He came down on the *Blade*, remember, and must've told Griff you were suspicious of there still being contraband hidden in the Conestogas. So Griff slaps a murder charge on you and locks you up . . . as far as he knows nothing has been found hidden in the wagons and it's on its way to be delivered – to whoever's waiting for it.'

Shannon was watching Connery steadily.

'We've passed through Customs, made five deliveries,' the cattle agent said slowly. 'And no one's expected any more than what they'd ordered – tools, casks of wine or tar or tallow, crates of canned goods. The contraband is still hidden in the Conestogas. No one's made any attempt to get it.'

'How many more deliveries have you got to make, Rube?' Connery asked quietly.

'Just one, Skipper – Hacienda Renaldo.'

Connery flicked his gaze to Shannon. 'Rennie admitted he stores stuff for this Salvadore, even has the man as a guest on occasion. . . .' He nodded suddenly. 'It's not so crazy to think he's mixed up with the rebs when you remember that El Presidente confiscated his entire herd of Arab-strain horses and hasn't paid him any compensation.'

'I can savvy that,' Shannon said slowly. 'But Glenda's there at the *hacienda* and that I can't abide.'

'No – I wouldn't say much around here in case that damn gunslinger Vibora hears you. He's mighty loyal to Rennie.'

'Hell, I don't care about Rennie being mixed up with Salvadore, but I don't want Glenda around there when the rebs come in to collect. It has to be the Gatling guns, Clay. The contraband in the wagons is a lot of parts for the guns: *essential parts*, breech covers, gears for the handles and so on. The guns must already be there somewhere.'

Connery frowned. 'Which means Salvadore must've known about the train hold-up to get the guns in the first place – likely even helped organize it. Yet he calls himself a pacifist . . . or tries to give that impression.'

'A mostly peaceful protest won't get anywhere with someone like the president, Clay – it'll have to be all-out war, or a damn big uprising. I mean, think about it – *eight* Gatling guns! Christ, it must be the president's worst nightmare to even think of them getting their hands on a *single* Gatling, let alone eight of them.'

Connery knew Shannon was right. 'But if those guns've got this far, Vinnie and maybe Keller, too, must've been paid for 'em. They wouldn't let 'em cross the Rio without getting their money first. A lot of money, too. It's obvious they held back the essential parts so they could hit Salvadore again for as much as the market will bear.' He looked up sharply. 'Would Rennie back Salvadore in something like that? I mean, Vinnie's out for a killing here. He'll want thousands and Glenda told me that Rennie is feeling the pinch, that he only has so many men still riding for him because of their loyalty. If it depended on paying their wages, they'd have quit long ago.'

'I think we better ask Rennie about that,' Shannon said tightly. 'And I want Glenda out of there as quickly as possible.'

'OK – Rube, can we load all the freight on to one wagon now, and combine what's left of the mules to pull it?'

Ruben pursed his lips. 'We-ell, might be enough for a team – and I guess there's plenty of men to handle the loadin'. . . .'

'Then let's get it done and move on.'

Connery was a little surprised at the feeling of urgency that had suddenly come over him.

And he was thinking about the girl, not the delivery.

CHAPTER 12

RIGHT SIDE OF
THE RIVER

There were no guards on the gate of Hacienda Renaldo.

Connery and Shannon, having ridden on ahead of the lumbering wagon, Vibora and his men even further back, with Ruben and McAllen bringing the Conestoga in, reined down. Connery turned to the cattle agent.

'This usual?'

Shannon shook his head, already sliding his rifle out of the saddle scabbard. 'Never seen Rennie's place unguarded before.'

Connery started to slide out his own rifle when the big door opened up at the white house. Don Renaldo appeared in his wheelchair, pushed by a strange white man.

'You will not need your guns, *amigos*,' called

143

Renaldo. 'Come on up to the house – Glenda is waiting.'

'Don't like this, Clay,' Shannon muttered slowly, sheathing his rifle again. Connery followed his lead, but he asked, 'You know that man pushing Rennie's chair?'

'Looked vaguely familiar – might've seen him in Brownsville.'

Connery tensed, but they rode up and dismounted and the man turned Renaldo's chair and pushed him back into the house, leaving the door open. Connery paused on the shaded porch and looked back through the gate's archway. There was dust out there and a slow-moving black shape. The Conestoga carrying the goods for the *hacienda* – and the Gatling gun parts. He wished now he hadn't told the *vaqueros* to take their time riding back – maybe they were too far back. He had the feeling they were going to need more back-up than just Ruben and the wounded McAllen.

They went through to the side patio where Renaldo waited with the strange *gringo* behind his chair. Glenda was seated in a leather-slung chair near the rail and two men moved out of the deep, cool shadow of the arched opening.

Griffin and Keller.

Shannon and Connery stopped in their tracks.

'Glenda! You all right?'

'Yes, Dad – no one's been harmed.'

'Yet,' said Griffin flatly, his hand resting on the butt of his Colt, hard eyes studying the new arrivals. 'I'll take delivery of those gun parts now, Connery.'

'Why didn't you take 'em in Brownsville?'

The sheriff shrugged. 'They had to be got across the border so I could deliver 'em. I knew Vinnie had hid 'em real well and made arrangements with the Customs. So I figured it was best to let the wagon pass through and then me and Kel came on down to collect.'

'You're a little late,' Connery said, and both men stiffened, eyes narrowing.

'Don't try anythin', Connery!' growled Keller, suddenly drawing his gun and stepping behind Renaldo's chair. He placed the muzzle against the rancher's temple. 'And we still have the girl!'

'Leave her out of this!' snapped Shannon, moving a hand towards his own sixgun.

Griffin's gun roared, filling the patio with a sudden thunder that dragged a stifled scream for Glenda. She came swiftly out of her chair as her father crashed back against the wall and slid down to one knee, head hanging as he reached out a shaky arm to steady himself against the adobe wall. He was bleeding from the right thigh. Griffin allowed her to kneel beside him, anxiously examining the wound, face anguished.

The sheriff looked steadily at Connery. 'Think it's about time we got this thing movin' along. We've gotta fix a meetin' with Salvadore yet and we don't want no delays. I've waited too long for this – Connery, you figure you can beat my draw, why you just have at it, pardner. I'd admire a chance to square-off with you.'

'Come on outside and we'll do it now,' offered

145

Clay, tightlipped. 'I win, your men ride on out; I lose. . . .' He shrugged.

Griffin smiled thinly, shook his head. 'Much as I'd like to, but I want them gun parts with no more delays! They're gonna make me rich.'

'Make *us* rich,' Keller corrected him.

'You two including Vinnie in this?' Connery watched as Glenda tended her father's wound with his neckerchief. She bound this over the wound tightly, for it was bleeding plenty. Shannon was pale and gritting his teeth against the pain. Keller still held his gun against Renaldo's head.

'Vinnie?' Griffin echoed, and pursed his lips, flicking his gaze towards Keller and smiling faintly. 'It was all Vinnie's idea, holdin' out the essential parts. . . .'

'You didn't answer the question.'

Griffin's smile widened and Keller chuckled. 'Have you forgotten already? You *killed* Vinnie after you escaped. Must've gone to his room to get money from him so you could get away and he resisted. You were seen goin' down the outside stairway of his hotel – reliable witness. Feller named Whiskey Jack Clute. He wanted to ride with us, but I told him to wait in town for us. Just in case we need his testimony.'

'Clute couldn't lie straight in bed,' Connery gritted and Griffin laughed.

Then Glenda was standing beside Connery. She clasped his arm. 'Oh, Clay!' It was his right arm and he prised her fingers loose, moved her around to his other side, pushing her behind his back. Griffin laughed again.

'You sure are cautious, Connery! But if you're

146

hopin' for a chance to out-smart me, forget it! Don
Renaldo will die first and then I'll finish you – or
maybe we'll kill the girl first, let you watch. Get it?'

Connery said nothing but the girl's grip tightened
and he heard her breath hiss through her nostrils.

'Son of a bitch's fixed you . . . good, Clay,' gritted
Shannon, fighting the pain in his leg. 'I think he . . .
busted the bone. . . .'

'Let me give him brandy!' Glenda appealed to
Griffin and the sheriff nodded towards the table
where the decanter stood. The girl poured some
liquor into a glass and knelt as she held it to her
father's lips, watched closely by Keller and Griffin.
The third *gringo* stood against the wall, arms folded,
and Shannon finally recognized him: he was Borden,
Vinnie's new bodyguard.

'Some bodyguard!' the cattle agent said gaspingly
after his drink, and Borden moved only his bullet
eyes in his head.

Glenda shivered.

Griffin chuckled. 'Bord's a good man – picked
him myself when Vinnie said he needed someone to
replace Brock.'

Connery knew now who had really killed Vinnie
Vincent – and framed him for the murder with a
bought-and-paid-for witness: Whiskey Clute, an old
vicious enemy.

'Now, Connery, why am I too late to pick up the
gun parts? I can see your wagon comin' across the
flats towards the gate right this minute.'

'We were hit by bandits, one called The Butcher,
Carnicero.'

That seemed to shock both Keller and the sheriff.

'Only one wagon, Griff?' Keller asked, unable to see the gate from his position behind Renaldo.

'Just one. Looks like a bunch of riders a fair way behind. *Vaqueros*.' Griffin threw a quizzical glance at Connery.

'Don Renaldo sent men with us – under Vibora. We beat off Carnicero but we ain't got all the gun parts.'

'You goddamn liar!' shouted Keller, screwing the gun muzzle into Renaldo's temple, hard enough to make the man writhe and gasp in pain.

Griffin walked across slowly and Connery pushed Glenda away a few paces. The sheriff stopped in front of them, glaring, then suddenly his left arm whipped out like a striking snake and Glenda cried out as she was dragged roughly in front of the crooked lawman. Griffin's right hand held his Colt, but it was aimed at the girl not Connery.

'I shot her old man in the leg – that won't matter much to him, he'll manage with a bit of a limp – but s'pose I was to shoot this here lovely's knee caps off? Beautiful young gal like her'd find life pretty damn hard, gettin' round on crutches or in a wheelchair. Likely never find anyone to marry her – not just because she'd be a cripple, but because I'd make sure her face would make a billygoat puke as well. . . .'

Glenda's breast was heaving as she breathed, her eyes wide and afraid. She was up on her tiptoes, body rigid with fear, appealing to Connery for help.

'Don't let him harm her, Clay!' gritted Shannon.

148

Connery didn't look at him. His gaze was fixed on Griffin. 'He knows he's dead an instant after he does anything to her.'

Griffin's face straightened at the chilling tone and the look on Connery's face. His trigger finger itched but something told him he was a hair away from death if he harmed the girl . . . but then his resolve hardened and he curled a lip.

'Up to you, big man! Get me them gun parts, or the lady spends her life on crutches!'

'For Christ's sake, Clay!' choked Shannon. 'Don't play with Glenda's life, damn you!'

'Griff,' said Keller suddenly. 'I can see the wagon now. Them Mexes're ridin' past it, comin' in ahead. Jesus, must be ten of 'em!'

Griffin turned to Don Renaldo but still holding the girl as a shield. 'You'd best go tell 'em to take a ride, Don Renaldo. They come up to the house and somebody's gonna get hurt. Bord, push him out to the porch and make sure he gives the right orders.'

Keller was reluctant to remove his gun from the *ranchero*'s head but allowed Borden to take the chair back and wheel Renaldo out to the front of the house. No one spoke, waited to hear what the rancher said.

The wagon was crunching gravel and rumbling through the archway, Ruben driving the weary, sweating mules, McAllen propped up beside him, bandage round his head and one arm in a rough sling.

'*Hola*, Vibora!' called Don Renaldo, lifting a hand in greeting. 'Señors Connery and Shannon have arrived – you will take the men up to the hills and start scouring them for mavericks. Make camp in Arroyo Salvar for the night. We will speak tomorrow.'

'Arroyo Salvar, *jefe*?' Vibora sounded puzzled.

'*Sí*, you know the one. Luis saw a big movement of cattle there this morning. I have sent him out to scout. You and your men can start gathering and building the holding corrals. Draw your stores and go there now.'

'At your command, *jefe*,' said the *segundo*.

Vibora still sounded perplexed to Connery, but the man obeyed orders and not long after the weary *vaqueros* turned and rode for the hills with their rack-slung supplies bouncing on the backs of mules.

The wagon was slowly lumbering up towards the front of the house and Connery could see Ruben frowning as the Mexicans rode back out through the gateway.

Renaldo called a greeting but pressure on his neck from Borden stopped him saying any more.

'Where you want this, *señor*?' asked Ruben, and Renaldo hipped around a little in the chair, looking back into the patio.

'Your orders, Señor Griffin?'

Ruben tensed and Griffin swore – the old man had outsmarted him there, warning Ruben and McAllen of his presence.

'Just bring in the gun parts, boy!' Griffin called.

He moved enough so Ruben could see he held the girl and Borden was already wheeling Renaldo back into the room.

'You in there, Skipper?' Ruben called, and Connery answered, ignoring the bleak warning

150

glance from Griffin.

'Better bring in what parts survived, Rube.'

Griffin swung around. '*Survived!* What the hell you playin' at now?'

'Told you we were attacked by Carnicero. We beat him off with help from Don Renaldo's *vaqueros*, but not before he'd set the second wagon on fire.'

For a moment, Connery thought Griffin was going to swing his gun on him and shoot him down. Then the sheriff said slowly, 'You're lyin'.'

Connery shrugged. 'Well, how many wagons d'you see out there? Look at the load – not even half as much as we had when we left Brownsville. And we only had two consignments for Matamoros. We couldn't save the other wagon, Griff. The heat was terrific – there were six barrels of pitch and some coal oil amongst the freight. When we scraped over the ashes all the gun parts had melted together – useless. That's what I meant when I said we don't have 'em all. At least half was lost in that fire.'

'Vinnie would've split the parts evenly!' shouted Keller, taking over from Borden and standing behind Renaldo's wheelchair again, gun aimed at the back of the man's head. 'I know him. Hell, he was careful as all get-out where makin' a dollar was concerned.'

'What d'you say, Connery?'

'Rube – you heard. Bring in what parts are in that wagon. We salvaged about six sets if I recollect.'

'Five, Skipper,' Rube replied easily, catching on smartly. 'One set was no good and we'd lost the screws anyway. They're useless without them special screws.'

151

Griffin didn't believe any of it. 'Bord – you go out there and bring in *all* the parts you see.'

Borden went outside without speaking, shoved Ruben's shoulder hard, sending him stumbling towards the wagon. McAllen put on a hangdog face, grimacing as he rubbed his head. 'I – feel kinda – dizzy.'

'Best climb down so you won't have so far to fall,' growled Borden, in a voice surpisingly thin for coming out of such a solid-looking man.

'Don't think I can – move,' Mac said, but Borden had lost interest now.

He pushed Ruben roughly towards the rear of the wagon. 'Get me them parts, boy.'

'You kiddin'? Hey, all this stuff has to be unloaded first before we can even get to where Vinnie hid the contraband! It's down in the wagonbed.'

Borden swore. 'You hear that, Griff?'

'Yeah – give him a hand and put that malingerer to work, too.'

'Aw, hell, Griff! I never signed on to unload freight wagons!'

'I want that load out of there in twenty minutes,' snapped Griffin. 'I don't care how it's done or who does it – just *get it out!*'

Grumbling, Borden helped Ruben drop the heavy tailgate and Ruben climbed up inside, stumbling over the stacked freight.

'You won't be able to lend a hand here, Mac, best climb down and come inside where it's cool,' called Connery.

'Yeah – I'll do that, Cap'n.' McAllen began to

struggle over the back of the driving seat, saying, 'Hope you're gonna pay for a sawbones to tend to me proper.'

'Yeah, I'll foot the bill, Mac. You want a hand to get down?'

Connery started forward but Griffin's gun came up and stopped him.

'Stay put!'

'I – I'll manage, Cap.' McAllen said, and he brought up his Colt and shot Borden off the back of the wagon, wrenching around with a grunt of pain, laying the gun on the shadowy men inside.

But he couldn't see who was who and then Borden, clinging to the back of the wagon with one arm, not yet dead, palmed up his sixgun and blazed two fast shots at McAllen, swung the smoking Colt to Rube who was wrestling with a heavy cask of tar. The bullet struck an iron band around the oak and Ruben dropped, got his boots against the curved staves and yelled with the effort of kicking the cask off the wagon.

Borden, body almost on the ground as he hung by one arm, blood on his shirt front, screamed as the heavy cask tumbled off and crushed him before rolling off his now misshapen body and out into the yard.

It all happened in seconds and Connery lunged for Griffin, but the man snapped a shot at him, pulled the girl in front of him and dragged her over the low patio rail.

Keller fired at Connery who was skidding on the tiled floor as he rolled, came round on to his belly, sixgun roaring its thunder in three rapid shots. Keller staggered and spun as the lead slammed home and he fell to one knee, eyes staring, his big square face slackening as he made one final effort to lift his gun and shoot Don Renaldo.

The *ranchero* rocked his chair wildly and it toppled sideways into Keller, knocking his gun hand aside so that the last shot the man fired went wild and screamed off the tiles, laying a silver streak across the terracotta.

'Rube! Get to Rennie! Mac all right?'

Rube straightened from bending over McAllen. 'No, Skipper – I think Borden's finished him.'

Connery, in the act of vaulting the low patio rail, paused, swore briefly. Then he made his leap and searched the yard swiftly for Griffin and Glenda.

A gun crashed and Connery dropped flat. A second shot kicked dirt into his face as he rolled in against the adobe wall, firing across his body as he glimpsed Griffin at the corner of the stables. Adobe dust erupted in a long line.

Then the sheriff came into full view, dragging a struggling Glenda with him. He cuffed her roughly, shook her, pulled her in front of him, and fired again at Connery. The bullet whined off the adobe and Griffin thumbed back his gun hammer but did not shoot.

'On your feet, Connery! And drop that Colt, or . . .'

He shook the girl and Connery set the Colt down on the ground and slowly stood up, hands out from his sides.

'I knew all that talk about a square-off between you and me was just hogwash,' he said, taunting. 'You know damn well you can't beat me.'

'That so?' sneered Griffin. 'Well, mebbe we'll see about that later, but right now, I want them gun parts! I've worked a damn long time to set this up.'

'Well, it's all yours now – if you can take it.'

'Kel's gone? Borden, too?' Griffin suddenly grinned. 'Hey, much obliged, Connery. You know, you're one hell of an *hombre*! Too bad we couldn't've gotten together. We'd make a damn good team.'

'No we wouldn't.'

Griffin sighed, absently shaking the girl who was very quiet and tense. 'No, guess not. Well, I was a good lawman for a long time but my wife got sick, you know? Lung fever – needed the real doctors back East, not these stitch-and-hack butchers we got on the frontier. Didn't have enough money. Everyone in Brownsville, and I mean bankers and rich river folk, would pat me on the back after I'd gunned down some wild son of a bitch of a rotgut-crazy cowpoke who was shootin' up the town, tell me what a fine job I was doin', but when it come to lendin' me money to send my wife to the Eastern doctors, they looked the other way, suddenly found chores to do out of town.'

Connery said nothing, but the girl had turned and was looking at the sheriff, still held tightly in his grip.

'So, I just had to watch her waste away. Didn't weigh much more'n forty pounds when she died. . . .' His voice drifted away and his face changed, suddenly pensive. Connery knew he was looking back down the long years to that tragedy that had turned him into the kind of man he was now – ready to kill an innocent girl if necessary just so long as he got his hands on those Gatling gun parts that would make him rich. . . . It was a twisted kind of revenge, he thought.

'How terrible for you,' Glenda said softly, and the sincerity in her voice was clear.

Griffin frowned. 'Huh?' He looked down at the girl, saw her compassionate face. 'Yeah – it was pretty awful . . . but I swore I'd get me some money from that time on, that I'd never be—'

'*Griff!*'

The voice came from behind and slightly above Connery. He was surprised to see the grey, pain-drawn face of Shannon as the man hooked one arm over the patio rail, the other hand, all bloodied, holding a pistol. He tried to raise it even as Griffin, still moving instinctively, eased up his grip briefly on the girl.

She wrenched free and flung herself away from the sheriff as Shannon, the effort proving too much for him, released his hold on the Colt and slid back to the tiles he had dragged himself across.

'Dad!' cried the girl, and started to run to him.

Griffin brought up his gun and Connery scooped up his own Colt off the ground, yelling, 'Now, Griff! *Now!*'

Griffin spun, shooting too fast, his lead spanging off the adobe house wall, and he threw himself back for the sheltering stables as he fired again. But Connery's shot mingled with that one and the sheriff staggered against the stable wall, slid down to one knee, gagging, turning his face towards Connery, bringing up his smoking gun again.

Connery triggered – but the Colt was empty.

Then a gun roared and Griffin shuddered, collapsing, shifting his gaze enough to see who had shot him.

Glenda, white-faced, held her father's gun in both hands and it sagged towards the ground as she sat down heavily and leaned her shoulders back against the adobe wall.

She began to cry as Connery came across, knelt on one knee and took the weapon from her hands. She turned to him, clutching at him, her body shuddering with her sobs.

Vibora and his men had come back and surrounded the *hacienda* because Don Renaldo's instructions to hold the mavericks in Arroyo Salvar – which meant 'rescue' – had told the Mexican all was not well in the big adobe house despite the don's assurance that it was.

'There is, of course, no Arroyo Salvar,' Renaldo explained later after everyone who needed it had had their wounds attended to and they were gathered in the big airy living-room. 'Vibora is an intelligent man – he knew what to do.'

'Well, I'd've been a lot happier if I'd known he was going to be coming back to rescue us,' Shannon said. He looked at Ruben who was sitting uncomfortably on the edge of a leather chair. 'Too bad about McAllen, Rube.'

The man nodded, looking at Connery. 'His last words, Skipper, were to get him a headstone like you bought for Ace.' Ruben smiled then. 'He said you could afford it.'

Connery smiled, too, nodded. 'Yeah, well, he's got it. But I won't be able to go back across the Rio for a spell.'

At their puzzled look, he added, 'Griff fixed me good with Vinnie's murder. Unless we can track down that "witness", Whiskey Clute, a man who hates my guts, I'm gonna have a time proving my innocence. So, looks like I stay on the wrong side of the river for some time yet. . . .'

Shannon agreed. 'I'll do what I can as soon as I get back, Clay. If Clute is still around I'll find him and clear your name.'

'Thanks, Yuma.' Connery turned to Don Renaldo. 'When's this Salvadore coming, Rennie?'

'He's already here.' They all looked at him, puzzled, and he laughed, spread his hands. 'Have you not guessed, *amigos?* I am Salvadore!'

'You? How can you be, Rennie, when the man travels all over Mexico. spreading his creed, recruiting followers.'

'If you were to ask people to describe the Salvador they saw and who spoke to them, who aroused their sense of justice, you would have a different description every time.' Don Renaldo smiled broadly. 'I instructed certain of my followers and they spread the word – no one could ever consider a man in a wheelchair as El Salvadore, the Saviour of the people!'

They had to admit he had a mighty good cover.

'And the big rebellion,' Connery asked quietly, 'it's coming soon? Now you have those Gatling guns, I mean.'

Sober now, Rennie nodded. 'Yes, my friend – very soon now. Presidente in his madness has started mass killing. It is time to use violence, I'm afraid. The guns have been here for quite some time, assembled, ready for action – except for those essential parts held back by Vinnie Vincenz and his friends. They demanded far more funds than I could raise for those parts, but I had to have the guns in working order. So I was thinking I would have to sell the *rancho*, but now. . . .' He swept his arm around the room. 'Thanks to you, my friends, I will soon be able to strike back at that tyrant.'

'Could you use an extra gun?' Connery asked, bringing surprise to all their faces. 'Well, I mean I've got to stay this side of the river until Yuma can clear my name . . . I don't mind fighting for a good cause.'

'And welcome you are, *amigo*!' said Don Renaldo. 'Most welcome.'

Ruben cleared his throat. 'I'm kinda used to workin' for the Cap'n now, Don Renaldo – I've had some trainin' on Gatlings. And I'm not bad with any kinda gun, you ask him.'

Connery confirmed it and Ruben was welcomed to Salvadore's band of *revolutionarios*, too.

'Well, looks like you and me're gonna have a lonely ride back to Texas, Glenda,' Shannon said, and then frowned as the girl came over and kissed him on the cheek.

159

'I am sure Don Renaldo will send Vibora or someone to keep you company on that long ride, Dad.'

'Now wait a minute! You can't—'

'Yes, I can, Dad,' Glenda said, standing beside the
stunned Connery, taking his hand. 'I want to be with
Clay – whatever side of the river he's on, is the right
side for me.'